Beyond

A Love Story

Elinor Glyn

Alpha Editions

This edition published in 2021

ISBN : 9789354844744

Design and Setting By
Alpha Editions
www.alphaedis.com
Email - info@alphaedis.com

As per information held with us this book is in Public Domain.
This book is a reproduction of an important historical work. Alpha Editions
uses the best technology to reproduce historical work in the same manner
it was first published to preserve its original nature. Any marks or number
seen are left intentionally to preserve its true form.

Beyond the Rocks

I

The hours were composed mostly of dull or rebellious moments during the period of Theodora's engagement to Mr. Brown. From the very first she had thought it hard that she should have had to take this situation, instead of Sarah or Clementine, her elder step-sisters, so much nearer his age than herself. To do them justice, either of these ladies would have been glad to relieve her of the obligation to become Mrs. Brown, but Mr. Brown thought otherwise.

A young and beautiful wife was what he bargained for.

To enter a family composed of three girls—two of the first family, one almost thirty and a second very plain—a father with a habit of accumulating debts and obliged to live at Bruges and inexpensive foreign sea-side towns, required a strong motive; and this Josiah Brown found in the deliciously rounded, white velvet cheek of Theodora, the third daughter, to say nothing of her slender grace, the grace of a young fawn, and a pair of gentian-blue eyes that said things to people in the first glance.

Poor, foolish, handsome Dominic Fitzgerald, light-hearted, débonair Irish gentleman, gay and gallant on his miserable pension of a broken and retired Guardsman, had had just sufficient sense to insist upon magnificent settlements, certainly prompted thereto by Clementine, who inherited the hard-headedness of the early defunct Scotch mother, as well as her high cheek-bones. That affair had been a youthful *mésalliance*.

"You had better see we all gain something by it, papa," she had said. "Make the old bore give Theodora a huge allowance, and have it all fixed and settled by law beforehand. She is such a fool about money—just like you—she will shower it upon us; and you make him pay you a sum down as well."

Captain Fitzgerald fortunately consulted an honest solicitor, and so things were arranged to the satisfaction of all parties concerned except Theodora herself, who found the whole affair far from her taste.

That one must marry a rich man if one got the chance, to help poor, darling papa, had always been part of her creed, more or less inspired by papa himself. But when it came to the scratch, and Josiah Brown was offered as a husband, Theodora had had to use every bit of her nerve and self-control to prevent herself from refusing.

She had not seen many men in her nineteen years of out-at-elbows life, but she had imagination, and the one or two peeps at smart old friends of papa's, landed from stray yachts now and then, at out-of-the-way French watering-places, had given her an ideal far, far removed from the personality of Josiah Brown.

But, as Sarah explained to her, such men could never be husbands. They might be lovers, if one was fortunate enough to move in their sphere, but husbands—never! and there was no use Theodora protesting this violent devotion to darling papa, if she could not do a small thing like marrying Josiah Brown for him!

Theodora's beautiful mother, dead in the first year of her runaway marriage, had been the daughter of a stiff-necked, unforgiving old earl; she had bequeathed her child, besides these gentian eyes and wonderful, silvery blond hair, a warm, generous heart and a more or less romantic temperament.

The heart was touched by darling papa's needs, and the romantic temperament revolted by Josiah Brown's personality.

However, there it was! The marriage took place at the Consulate at Dieppe, and a perfectly miserable little bride got into the train for Paris, accompanied by a fat, short, prosperous, middle-class English husband, who had accumulated a large fortune in Australia, quite by accident, in a comparatively few years.

Josiah Brown was only fifty-two, though his head was bald and his figure far from slight. He had a liver, a chest, and a temper, and he adored Theodora.

Captain Fitzgerald had felt a few qualms when he had wished his little daughter good-bye on the platform and had seen the blue stars swimming with tears. The two daughters left to him were so plain, and he hated plain people about him; but, on the other hand, women must marry, and what chance had he, poor, unlucky devil, of establishing his Theodora better in life?

Josiah Brown was a good fellow, and he, Dominic Fitzgerald, had for the first time for many years a comfortable balance at his bankers, and could run up to Paris himself in a few days, and who knows, the American widow, fabulously rich—Jane Anastasia McBride—might take him seriously!

Captain Dominic Fitzgerald was irresistible, and had that fortunate knack of looking like a gentleman in the oldest clothes. If married for the third time—but this time prosperously, to a fabulously rich American—his well-born relations would once more welcome him with open arms, he felt sure, and visions of the best pheasant shoots at old Beechleigh, and partridge drives at Rothering Castle floated before his eyes, quite obscuring the fading smoke of the Paris train.

"A pretty tough, dull affair marriage," he said to himself, reminded once more of Theodora by treading on a white rose in the station. "Hope to Heavens Sarah prepared her for it a bit." Then he got into a *fiacre* and drove to the hotel, where he and the two remaining Misses Fitzgerald were living in the style of their forefathers.

Josiah Brown's valet, Mr. Toplington, who knew the world, had engaged rooms for the happy couple at the Grand Hotel. "We'll go to the Ritz on our way back," he decided, "but at first, in case there's scenes and tears, it's better to be a number than a name." Mademoiselle Henriette, the freshly engaged French maid, quite agreed with him. The Grand, she said, was "*plus convenable pour une lune de Miel*—" Lune de Miel!

II

It was a year later before Theodora saw her family again. A very severe attack of bronchitis, complicated by internal catarrh, prostrated Josiah Brown in the first days of their marriage, and had turned her into a superintendent nurse for the next three months; by that time a winter at Hyères was recommended by the best physicians, and off they started.

Hyères, with a semi-invalid, a hospital nurse, and quantities of medicine bottles and draught-protectors, is not the ideal place one reads of in guide-books. Theodora grew to hate the sky and the blue Mediterranean. She used to sit on her balcony at Costebelle and gaze at the olive-trees, and the deep-green velvet patch of firs beyond, towards the sea, and wonder at life.

She longed to go to the islands—anywhere beyond—and one day she read *Jean d'Agrève*; and after that she wondered what Love was. It took a mighty hold upon her imagination. It seemed to her it must mean Life.

It was the beginning of May before Josiah Brown thought of leaving for Paris. England would be their destination, but the doctors assured him a month of Paris would break the change of climate with more safety than if they crossed the Channel at once.

Costebelle was a fairyland of roses as they drove to the station, and peace had descended upon Theodora. She had fallen into her place, a place occupied by many wives before her with irritable, hypochondriacal husbands.

She had often been to Paris in her maiden days; she knew it from the point of view of a cheap boarding-house and snatched meals. But the unchecked gayety of the air and the *façon* had not been tarnished by that. She had played in the Tuilleries Gardens and watched Ponchinello at the Rond Point, and later been taken once or twice to dine at a cheap café in the Bois by papa. And once she had gone to Robinson on a coach with him and some aristocratic acquaintances of his, and eaten luncheon up the tree, and that was a day of the gods and to be remembered.

But now they were going to an expensive, well-managed private hotel in the Avenue du Bois, suitable to invalids, and it poured with rain as they drove from the Gare de Lyon.

"She Wondered What Love Was."

All this time something in Theodora was developing. Her beautiful face had an air of dignity. The set of her little Greek head would have driven a sculptor wild—and Josiah Brown was very generous in money matters, and she had always known how to wear her clothes, so it was no wonder people stopped and turned their heads when she passed.

Josiah Brown possessed certainly not less than forty thousand a year, and so felt he could afford a carriage in Paris, and any other fancy he pleased. His nerves had been too shaken by his illness to appreciate the joys of an automobile.

Thus, daily might be seen in the Avenue des Acacias this ill-assorted pair, seated in a smart victoria with stepping horses, driving slowly up and down. And a number of people took an interest in them.

Towards the middle of May Captain Fitzgerald arrived at the Continental, and Theodora felt her heart beat with joy when she saw his handsome, well-groomed head.

Oh yes, it had been indeed worth while to make papa look so prosperous as that—so prosperous and happy—dear, gay papa!

He was about the same age as her husband, but no one would think of taking him for more than forty. And what a figure he had! and what manners! And when he patted her cheek Theodora felt at once that thrill of pride and gratification she had always experienced when he was pleased with her, from her youngest days.

She was almost glad Sarah and Clementine should have remained at Dieppe. Thus she could have papa all to herself, and oh, what presents she would send them back by him when he returned!

Josiah Brown despised Dominic Fitzgerald, and yet stood in awe of him as well. A man who could spend a fortune and be content to live on odds and ends for the rest of his life must be a poor creature. But, on the other hand, there was that uncomfortable sense of breeding about him which once, when Captain Fitzgerald had risen to a situation of dignity during their preliminary conversations about Theodora's hand, had made Josiah Brown unconsciously say "Sir" to him.

He had blushed and bitten his tongue for doing it, and had blustered and patronized immoderately afterwards, but he never forgot the incident. They were not birds of a feather, and never would be, though the exquisite manners of Dominic Fitzgerald could carry any situation.

Josiah was not altogether pleased to see his father-in-law. He even experienced a little jealousy. Theodora's face, which generally wore a mask of gentle, solicitous meekness for him, suddenly sparkled and rippled with laughter, as she pinched her papa's ears, and pulled his mustache, and purred into his neck, with joy at their meeting.

It was that purring sound and those caressing tricks that Josiah Brown objected to. He had never received any of them himself, and so why should Dominic Fitzgerald?

Captain Fitzgerald, for his part, was enchanted to clasp his beautiful daughter once more in his arms; he had always loved Theodora, and when he saw her so quite too desirable-looking in her exquisite clothes, he felt a very fine fellow himself, thinking what he had done for her.

It was not an unnatural circumstance that he should look upon the idea of a dinner at the respectable private hotel, with his son-in-law and daughter, as a trifle dull for Paris, or that he should have suggested a meal at the Ritz would do them both good.

"Come and dine with me instead, my dear child," he said, with his grand air. "Josiah, you must begin to go out a little and shake off your illness, my dear fellow."

But Josiah was peevish.

Not to-night—certainly not to-night. It was the evening he was to take the two doses of his new medicine, one half an hour after the other, and he could not leave the hotel. Then he saw how poor Theodora's face fell, and one of his sparks of consideration for the feelings of others came to him, and he announced gruffly that his wife might go with her father, if she pleased, provided she crept into her room, which was next door to his own, without the least noise on her return.

"I must not be disturbed in my first sleep," he said; and Theodora thanked him rapturously.

It was so good of him to let her go—she would, indeed, make not the least noise, and she danced out of the room to get ready in a way Josiah Brown had never seen her do before. And after she had gone—Captain Fitzgerald came back to fetch her—this fact rankled with him and prevented his sleep for more than twenty minutes.

"My sweet child," said Captain Fitzgerald, when he was seated beside his daughter in her brougham, rolling down the Champs-Elysées, "you must not be so grateful; he won't let you out again if you are."

"Oh, papa!" said Theodora.

They arrived at the Ritz just at the right moment. It was a lovely night, but rather cold, so there were no diners in the garden, and the crowd from the restaurant extended even into the hall.

It was an immense satisfaction to Dominic Fitzgerald to walk through them all with this singularly beautiful young woman, and to remark the effect she produced, and his cup of happiness was full when they came upon a party at the lower end by the door; prominent, as hostess, being Jane Anastasia McBride—the fabulously rich American widow.

In a second of time he reviewed the situation; a faint coldness in his manner would be the thing to draw—and it was; for when he had greeted Mrs. McBride without gush, and presented his daughter with the air of just passing on, the widow implored them with great cordiality to leave their solitary meal and join her party. Nor would she hear of any refusal.

The whole scene was so novel and delightful to Theodora she cared not at all whether her father accepted or no, so long as she might sit quietly and observe the world.

Mrs. McBride had perceived immediately that the string of pearls round Mrs. Josiah Brown's neck could not have cost less than nine thousand pounds, and that her frock, although so simple, was the last and most expensive creation of Callot Sœurs. She had always been horribly attracted by Captain Fitzgerald, ever since that race week at Trouville two summers ago, and fate had sent them here to-night, and she meant to enjoy herself.

Captain Fitzgerald acceded to her request with his usual polished ease, and the radiant widow presented the rest of her guests to the two new-comers.

The tall man with the fierce beard was Prince Worrzoff, married to her niece, Saidie Butcher. Saidie Butcher was short, and had a voice you could hear across the room. The sleek, fair youth with the twinkling gray eyes was an Englishman from the Embassy. The disagreeable-looking woman in the badly made mauve silk was his sister, Lady Hildon. The stout, hook-nosed bird of prey with the heavy gold chain was a Western millionaire, and the smiling girl was his daughter. Then, last of all, came Lord Bracondale—and it was when he was presented that Theodora first began to take an interest in the party.

Hector, fourteenth Lord Bracondale of Bracondale (as she later that night read in the *Peerage*) was aged thirty-one years. He had been educated at Eton and Oxford, served for some time in the Fourth Lifeguards, been unpaid attaché at St. Petersburg, was patron of five livings, and sat in the House of Lords as Baron Bracondale; creation, 1505; seat, Bracondale Chase. Brothers, none. Sister living, Anne Charlotte, married to the fourth Earl of Anningford.

Theodora read all this over twice, and also even the predecessors and collateral branches—but that was while she burned the midnight oil and listened to the snorts and coughs of Josiah Brown, slumbering next door.

For the time being she raised her eyes and looked into Lord Bracondale's, and something told her they were the nicest eyes she had ever seen in this world.

Then when a voluble French count had rushed up, with garrulous apologies for being late, the party was complete, and they swept into the restaurant.

Theodora sat between the Western millionaire and the Russian Prince, but beyond—it was a round table, only just big enough to hold them—came her hostess and Lord Bracondale, and two or three times at dinner they spoke, and very often she felt his eyes fixed upon her.

Mrs. McBride, like all American widows, was an admirable hostess; the conversation never flagged, or the gayety for one moment.

The Western millionaire was shrewd, and announced some quaint truths while he picked his teeth with an audible sound.

"This is his first visit to Europe," Princess Worrzoff said afterwards to Theodora by way of explanation. "He is so colossally rich he don't need to worry about such things at his time of life; but it does make me turn to hear him."

Captain Fitzgerald was in his element. No guest shone so brilliantly as he. His wit was delicate, his sallies were daring, his looks were insinuating, and his appearance was perfection.

Theodora had every reason to tingle with pride in him, and the widow felt her heart beat.

"Isn't he just too bright—your father, Mrs. Brown?" she said as they left the restaurant to have their coffee in the hall. "You must let me see quantities of you while we are all in Paris together. It is a lovely city; don't you agree with me?"

And Theodora did.

Lord Bracondale was of the same breed as Captain Fitzgerald—that is, they neither of them permitted themselves to be superseded by any other man with the object of their wishes. When they wanted to talk to a woman they did, if twenty French counts or Russian princes stood in the way! Thus it was that for the rest of the evening Theodora found herself seated upon a sofa in close proximity to the man who had interested her at dinner, and Mrs. McBride and Captain Fitzgerald occupied two arm-chairs equally well placed, while the rest of the party made general conversation.

Hector Bracondale, among other attractions, had a charming voice; it was deep and arresting, and he had a way of looking straight into the eyes of the person he was talking to.

Theodora knew at once he belonged to the tribe whom Sarah had told her could never be husbands.

She wondered vaguely why, all the time she was talking to him. Why had husbands always to be bores and unattractive, and sometimes even simply revolting, like hers? Was it because these beautiful creatures could not be bound to any one woman? It seemed to her unsophisticated mind that it could be very nice to be married to one of them; but there was no use fighting against fate, and she personally was wedded to Josiah Brown.

Lord Bracondale's conversation pleased her. He seemed to understand exactly what she wanted to talk about; he saw all the things she saw and—he had read *Jean d'Agrève!*—they got to that at the end of the first half-hour, and then she froze up a little; some instinct told her it was dangerous ground, so she spoke suddenly of the weather, in a banal voice.

Meanwhile, from the beginning of dinner, Lord Bracondale had been saying to himself she was the loveliest white flower he had yet struck in a path of varied experiences. Her eyes so innocent and true, with the tender expression of a fawn; the perfect turn of her head and slender pillar of a throat; her grace and gentleness, all appealed to him in a maddening way.

"She is asleep to the whole of life's possibilities," he thought. "What can her husband be about, and *what* an intoxicatingly agreeable task to wake her up!"

He had lived among the world where the awaking of young wives, or old wives, or any woman who could please man, was the natural course of the day. It never even struck him then it might be a cruel thing to do. A woman once married was always fair game; if the husband could not retain her affections that was his lookout.

Hector Bracondale was not a brute, just an ordinary Englishman of the world, who had lived and loved and seen many lands.

He read Theodora like an open book: he knew exactly why she had talked about the weather after *Jean d'Agrève*. It thrilled him to see her soft eyes dreamy and luminous when they first spoke of the book, and it flattered him when she changed the conversation.

As for Theodora, she analyzed nothing, she only felt that perhaps she ought not to speak about love to one of those people who could never be husbands.

Captain Fitzgerald, meanwhile, was making tremendous headway with the widow. He flattered her vanity, he entertained her intelligence, and he even ended by letting her see she was causing him, personally, great emotion.

At last this promising evening came to an end. The Russian Prince, with his American Princess, got up to say good-night, and gradually the party broke up, but not before Captain Fitzgerald had arranged to meet Mrs.

McBride at Doucet's in the morning, and give her the benefit of his taste and experience in a further shopping expedition to buy old bronzes.

"We can all breakfast together at Henry's," he said, with his grand manner, which included the whole party; and for one instant force of habit made Theodora's heart sink with fear at the prospect of the bill, as it had often had to do in olden days when her father gave these royal invitations. Then she remembered she had not been sacrificed to Josiah Brown for nothing, and that even if dear, generous papa should happen to be a little hard up again, a few hundred francs would be nothing to her to slip into his hand before starting.

The rest of the party, however, declined. They were all busy elsewhere, except Lord Bracondale and the French Count—they would come, with pleasure, they said.

Theodora wondered what Josiah would say. Would he go? and if not, would he let her go? This was more important.

"Then we shall meet at breakfast to-morrow," Lord Bracondale said, as he helped her on with her cloak. "That will give me something to look forward to."

"Will it?" she said, and there was trouble in the two blue stars which looked up at him. "Perhaps I shall not be able to come; my husband is rather an invalid, and—"

But he interrupted her.

"Something tells me you will come; it is fate," he said, and his voice was grave and tender.

And Theodora, who had never before had the opportunity of talking about destiny, and other agreeable subjects, with beautiful Englishmen who could only be—lovers—felt the red blood rush to her cheeks and a thrill flutter her heart. So she quickened her steps and kept close to her father, who could have dispensed with this mark of affection.

"Dearest child," he said, when they were seated in the brougham, "you are married now and should be able to look after yourself, without staying glued to my side so much—it is rather bourgeois."

Poor Theodora was crushed and did not try to excuse herself.

"I am afraid Josiah won't go, papa dear," she said, timidly; "and in case he does not allow me to either, I want you to have these few louis, just for the breakfast. I know how generous you are, and how difficult things have been made for you, darling." And she nestled to his side and slipped about eight gold pieces, which she had fortunately found in her purse, into his hand.

Captain Fitzgerald was still a gentleman, although a good many edges of his sensitive perceptions had been rubbed off.

He kissed his daughter fondly while he murmured: "Merely a loan, my pet, merely a loan. You were always a jewel to your old father!"

Whenever her parent accused himself of being "old," Theodora knew he was deeply touched, and her tender heart overflowed with gladness that she was able to smooth the path of such a darling papa.

"I will come and see you in the morning, my child," he said, as they stopped at the door of her hotel, "and I will manage Josiah."

So Theodora crept up to her apartment, comforted; and in the salon it was she caught sight of the *Peerage*.

Josiah Brown bought one every year and travelled with it, although until he met the Fitzgerald family he had not known a single person connected with it; but it pleased him to be able to look up his wife's name, and to read that her mother was the daughter of a real live earl and her father the brother of a baronet.

"Hector! I like the name of Hector," were the last coherent thoughts which floated through the brain of Theodora before sleep closed her broad, white lids.

Meanwhile, Lord Bracondale had gone on to sup at the Café de Paris, with Marion de Beauvoison and Esclarmonde de Chartres; and among the diamonds and pearls and scents and feathers he suddenly felt a burning disgust, and a longing to be out again in the moonlight—alone with his thoughts.

"Mais qu'as tu, mon vieux chou?" they said. "Ce bel Hector chéri—il a un béguin pour quelqu'un—mais ce n'est pas pour nous autres!"

III

Josiah Brown cut the top off his *œuf à la coque* with a knife at his *premier déjeuner* next day. The knife grated on the shell in a determined way, and Theodora felt her heart sink at the prospect of broaching the subject of the breakfast at the Café Henry.

"I am so glad the rain has stopped," she said, nervously. "It was raining when I woke this morning."

"Indeed," replied Josiah. "And what kind of an evening did you pass with that father of yours?"

"A very pleasant one," said Theodora, crumbling her roll. "Papa met some old friends, and we all dined together at the Ritz. I wish you had been able to come, it might have done you good, it was so gay!"

"I am not fit for gayety," said her husband, peevishly, scooping out spoonfuls of yolk. "And who were the party, pray?"

Theodora obediently enumerated them all, and the high-sounding title of the Russian Prince, to say nothing of the English lord and lady, had a mollifying effect on Josiah Brown. He even remembered the name of Bracondale—had he not been a grocer's assistant in the small town of Bracondale for a whole year in his apprenticeship days?

"Papa wants us to breakfast to-day with him at Henry's for you to meet some of them," Theodora said, with more confidence.

Josiah had taken a second egg and his frown was gone.

"We'll see about it, we'll see about it," he grunted; but his wife felt more hopeful, and was even unusually solicitous of his wants in the way of coffee and marmalade and cream. Josiah was shrewd if he did happen to be deeply self-absorbed in his health, and he noticed that Theodora's eyes were brighter and her step more elastic than usual.

He knew he had bought "one of them there aristocrats," as his old aunt, who had kept a public-house at New Norton, would have said. Bought her with solid gold—he had no illusions on this subject, and he quite realized if the solid gold had not been amassed out of England, so that to her family he could be represented as "something from the colonies—rather rough, but such a good fellow"—even Captain Fitzgerald's impecuniosity and rapacity would not have risen to his bait.

He was also grateful to Theodora—she had been so meek always, and such a kind and unselfish nurse. With his impaired constitution and delicate chest he had given up all hopes of looking on her as a wife again, just yet; but, as a nurse and an ornament—a peg to hang the evidences of his wealth upon—she was little short of perfection. He could have been frantically in love with her if she had only been the girl from the station bar in Melbourne. Josiah Brown was not a bad fellow.

By the time Mr. Toplington advanced in his dignified way with the accurately measured tonic on a silver tray and the single acid drop to remove the taste, Josiah Brown had decided to go and partake food with his father-in-law at Henry's. If he had been good enough to entertain the Governor of Australia, he was quite good enough for Russian princes or English lords, he told himself. Thus it was that Captain Fitzgerald, who came in person in a few minutes to indorse his invitation, found an unusually cordial reception awaiting him.

"I am too delighted, my dear Josiah," he said, "that you have decided to come out of your shell. Moping would kill a cat; and I shall order you the plainest chicken and soufflé aux fraises."

"Josiah can eat almost anything, papa. I don't think you need worry about that," said Theodora, who hoped to make her husband enjoy himself. And then Captain Fitzgerald left to meet his widow.

All the morning, while she walked up and down under the trees in the Avenue du Bois beside her husband, who leaned upon her arm, Theodora's thoughts were miles away. She felt stimulated, excited, intensely interested in the hour, afraid they would be late. Twice she answered at random, and Josiah got quite cross.

"I asked you which you considered would do me most good when we return to England, to continue seeing Sir Baldwin once a week or to have Dr. Wilton permanently in the house with us, and you answer that you quite agree with me! Agree with what? Agree with which? You are talking nonsense, girl!"

Theodora apologized gently, and her white velvet cheeks became tinged with wild roses. It seemed as if the victoria, with its high-steppers, would never come and pick them up; and it must be at least quarter of an hour's drive to Henry's. She did not understand where it was exactly, but papa had said the coachman would know.

If some one had told her, as Clementine certainly would have done had she been there, that she was simply thus interested and excited because she wished to see again Lord Bracondale, she would have been horrified. She never had analyzed sensations herself, and the day had not yet arrived when she would begin to do so.

At last they were rolling down the Champs-Elysées. The mass of chestnut blooms in full glory, the tender green still fresh and springlike, the sky as blue as blue, and every creature in the street with an air of gayety—that Paris alone seems to inspire in the human race. It entered into her blood, this rush of spring and hope and laughter and life, and a radiant creature got out of the carriage at Henry's door.

The two men were waiting for them—Lord Bracondale and the French Count—her father and Mrs. McBride had not yet appeared.

Theodora introduced them to her husband, and Lord Bracondale said:

"Mrs. McBride is always late. I have found out which is your father's table; don't you think we might go and sit down?"

And they did. Theodora got well into the corner of the velvet sofa, the Count on one side and Lord Bracondale on the other, with Josiah beyond the Count.

They made conversation. The Frenchman was voluble and agreeable, and the next ten minutes passed without incident.

Josiah, not quite at ease, perhaps, but on the whole not ill-pleased with his situation. The Count took all ups and downs as of the day's work, sure of a good breakfast, sooner or later, unpaid for by himself. And Lord Bracondale's thoughts ran somewhat thus:

"She is even more beautiful in daylight than at night. She can't be more than twenty—what a skin! like a white gardenia petal—and, good Lord, what a husband! How revolting, how infamous! I suppose that old schemer, her father, sold her to him. Her eyes remind one of forgotten fairy tales of angels. Can anything be so sweet as that little nose and those baby-red lips. She has a soul, too, peeping out of the blue when she looks up at one. She reminds me of Praxiteles' Psyche when she looks down. Why did I not meet her long ago? I believe I ought not to stay now—something tells me I shall fall deeply into this. And what a voice!—as gentle and caressing as a tender dove. A man would give his soul for such a woman. As guileless as an infant saint, too— and sensitive and human and understanding. I wish to God I had the strength of mind to get up and go this minute—but I haven't—it is fate."

"Oh, how naughty of papa," said Theodora, "to be so late! Are you very hungry, Josiah? Shall we begin without them?"

But at that moment, with rustling silks and delicate perfume, the widow and Captain Fitzgerald came in at the door and joined the party.

"I am just too sorry," the lady said, gayly. "It is all Captain Fitzgerald's fault—he would try to restrain me from buying what I wanted, and so it made me obstinate and I had to stay right there and order half the shop."

"How I understand you!" sympathized Lord Bracondale. "I know just that feeling of wanting forbidden fruit. It makes the zest of life."

He had foreseen the disposition of the party, and by sitting in the outside corner seat at the end knew he would have Theodora almost *en tête-à-tête*, once they were all seated along the velvet sofa beyond Josiah Brown.

"What do you do with yourself all the time here?" he asked, lowering his voice to that deep note which only carries to the ear it is intended for. "May one ever see you again except at a chance meal like this?"

"I don't know," said Theodora. "I walk up and down in the side allées of the Bois in the morning with my husband, and when he has had his sleep, after déjeuner, we drive nearly all the afternoon, and we have tea, at the Pré Catalan and drive again until about seven, and then we come in and dine, and I go to bed very early. Josiah is not strong enough yet for late hours or theatres."

"It sounds supernaturally gay for Paris!" said Lord Bracondale; and then he felt a brute when he saw the cloud in the blue eyes.

"No, it is not gay," she said, simply. "But the flowers are beautiful, and the green trees and the chestnut blossoms and the fine air here, and there is a little stream among the trees which laughs to itself as it runs, and all these things say something to me."

He felt rebuked—rebuked and interested.

"I would like to see them all with you," he said.

That was one of his charms—directness. He did not insinuate often; he stated facts.

"You would find it all much too monotonous," she answered. "You would tire of them after the first time. And you could if you liked, too, because I suppose you are free, being a man, and can choose your own life," and she sighed unconsciously.

And there came to Hector Bracondale the picture of her life—sacrificed, no doubt, to others' needs. He seemed to see the long years tied to Josiah Brown, the cramping of her soul, the dreary desolation of it. Then a tenderness came over him, a chivalrous tenderness unfelt by him towards women now for many a long day.

"I wonder if I can choose my life," he said, and he looked into her eyes.

"Why can you not?" She hesitated. "And may I ask you, too, what you do with yourself here?"

He evaded the question; he suddenly realized that his days were not more amusing than hers, although they were filled up with racing and varied employments—while the thought of his nights sickened him.

"I think I am going to make an immense change and learn to take pleasure in the running brooks," he said. "Will you help me?"

"I know so little, and you know so much," and her sweet eyes became soft and dreamy. "I could not help you in any way, I fear."

"Yes, you could—you could teach me to see all things with fresh eyes. You could open the door into a new world."

"Do you know," she said, irrelevantly, "Sarah—my eldest sister—Sarah told me it was unwise ever to talk to strangers except in the abstract—and here are you and I conversing about our own interests and feelings—are not we foolish!" She laughed a little nervously.

"No, we are not foolish because we are not strangers—we never were—and we never will be."

"Are not strangers—?"

"No—do you not feel that sometimes in life one's friendships begin by antipathy—sometimes by indifference—and sometimes by that sudden magnetism of sympathy as if in some former life we had been very near and dear, and were only picking up the threads again, and to such two souls there is no feeling that they are strangers."

Theodora was too entirely unsophisticated to remain unmoved by this reasoning. She felt a little thrill—she longed to continue the subject, and yet dared not. She turned hesitatingly to the Count, and for the next ten minutes Lord Bracondale only saw the soft outline of her cheek.

He wondered if he had been too sudden. She was quite the youngest person he had ever met—he realized that, and perhaps he had acted with too much precipitation. He would change his tactics.

The Count was only too pleased to engage the attention of Theodora. He was voluble; she had very little to reply. Things went smoothly. Josiah was appreciating an exceedingly good breakfast, and the playful sallies of the fair widow. All, in fact, was *couleur de rose*.

"Won't you talk to me any more?" Lord Bracondale said, after about a quarter of an hour. He felt that was ample time for her to have become calm, and, beautiful as the outline of her cheek was, he preferred her full face.

"But of course," said Theodora. She had not heard more than half what the Count had been saying; she wished vaguely that she might continue the subject of friendship, but she dared not.

"Do you ever go to Versailles?" he asked. This, at least, was a safe subject.

"I have been there—but not since—not this time," she answered. "I loved it: so full of memories and sentiment, and Old-World charm."

"It would give me much pleasure to take you to see it again," he said, with grave politeness. "I must devise some plan—that is, if you wish to go."

She smiled.

"It is a favorite spot of mine, and there are some alleés in the park more full of the story of spring than your Bois even."

"I do not see how we can go," said Theodora. "Josiah would find it too long a day."

"I must discuss it with your father; one can generally arrange what one wishes," said Lord Bracondale.

At this moment Mrs. McBride leaned over and spoke to Theodora. She had, she said, quite converted Mr. Brown. He only wanted a little cheering up to be perfectly well, and she had got him to promise to dine that evening at Armenonville and listen to the Tziganes. It was going to be a glorious night, but if they felt cold they could have their table inside out of the draught. What did Theodora think about it?

Theodora thought it would be a delicious plan. What else could she think?

"I have a large party coming," Mrs. McBride said, "and among them a compatriot of mine who saw you last night and is dying to meet you."

"Really," said Theodora, unmoved.

Lord Bracondale experienced a sensation of annoyance.

"I shall not ask you, Bracondale," the widow continued, playfully. "Just to assert British superiority, you would try to monopolize Mrs. Brown, and my poor Herryman Hoggenwater would have to come in a long, long second!"

Josiah felt a rush of pride. This brilliant woman was making much of his meek little wife.

Lord Bracondale smiled the most genial smile, with rage in his heart.

"I could not have accepted in any case, dear lady," he said, "as I have some people dining with me, and, oddly enough, they rather suggested they wanted

Armenonville too, so perhaps I shall have the pleasure of looking at you from the distance."

The conversation then became general, and soon after this coffee arrived, and eventually the adieux were said.

Mrs. McBride insisted upon Theodora accompanying her in her smart automobile.

"You leave your wife to me for an hour," she said, imperiously, to Josiah, "and go and see the world with Captain Fitzgerald. He knows Paris."

"My dear, you are just the sweetest thing I have come across this side of the Atlantic," she said, when they were whizzing along in her car. "But you look as if you wanted cheering too. I expect your husband's illness has worried you a good deal."

Theodora froze a little. Then she glanced at the widow's face and its honest kindliness melted her.

"Yes, I have been anxious about him," she said, simply, "but he is nearly well now, and we shall soon be going to England."

Mrs. McBride had not taken a companion on this drive for nothing, and she obtained all the information she wanted during their tour in the Bois. How Josiah Brown had bought a colossal place in the eastern counties, and intended to have parties and shoot there in the autumn. How Theodora hoped to see more of her sisters than she had done since her marriage. The question of these sisters interested Mrs. McBride a good deal.

For a man to have two unmarried daughters was rather an undertaking.

What were their ages—their habits—their ambitions? Theodora told her simply. She guessed why she was being interrogated. She wished to assist her father, and to say the truth seemed to her the best way. Sarah was kind and humorous, while Clementine had the brains.

"And they are both dears," she said, lovingly, "and have always been so good to me."

Mrs. McBride was a shrewd woman, full of American quickness, lightning deduction, and a phenomenal insight into character. Theodora seemed to her to be too tender a flower for this world of east wind. She felt sure she only thought good of every one, and how could one get on in life if one took that view habitually! The appallingly hard knocks fate would give one if one was so trusting! But as the drive went on that gentle something that seemed to emanate from Theodora, the something of pure sweetness and light, affected her, too, as it affected other people. She felt she was looking into a deep pool of crystal water, so deep that she could see no bottom or fathom the distance of it, but which reflected in brilliant blue God's sky and the sun.

"And she is by no means stupid," the widow summed up to herself. "Her mind is as bright as an American's! And she is just too pretty and sweet to be eaten up by these wolves of men she will meet in England, with that unromantic, unattractive husband along. I must do what I can for her."

By the time she had dropped Theodora at her hotel the situation was quite clear. Of course the girl had been sacrificed to Josiah Brown; she was sound asleep in the great forces of life; she was bound to be hideously unhappy, and it was all an abominable shame, and ought to have been prevented.

But Mrs. McBride never cried over spilled milk.

"If I decide to marry her father," she thought, as she drove off, "I shall keep my eye on her, and meanwhile I can make her life smile a little perhaps!"

IV

Theodora did not wonder why she felt in no exalted state of spirits as she dressed for dinner. She seldom thought of herself at all, or what her emotions were, but the fact remained there was none of the excitement there had been over the prospect of breakfast. Her husband, on the contrary, seemed quite fussy.

"A devilish fine woman," he had described Mrs. McBride. "Acts like a tonic upon me; does me more good than a pint of champagne!"

"Is she not delightful?" agreed Theodora; "so very kind and gay. I am sure the dinner will do you good, Josiah, and perhaps we might give one in return. What do you say?"

Josiah said, "Certainly!" He could give a meal with the best of them! They would consult that father of hers, who knew Paris so well, and ask him to help them to arrange a regular "slap-up treat."

And so they arrived at Armenonville. It was a divine night, quite warm, and a soft three-quarter moon.

Mrs. McBride had everything arranged to perfection. Their table was just where it should be, the menu was all that heart of gourmet could desire, and the company sparkling.

Theodora found herself seated beside Mr. Harryman Hoggenwater and an elderly Austrian, and before the *hors d'œuvres* were cleared away both gentlemen had decided to make love to her.

It was when the *bisque d'écrevisses* was being handed she became conscious that, not two tables off, there was an empty one simply arranged with flowers, and almost at the same instant Lord Bracondale and his party arrived upon the scene.

All Theodora's perceptions seemed to be sharpened. She knew without turning her head the table was for them, and that they were advancing towards it. She had felt their arrival almost before their automobile stopped; and now she would not look up.

A strange sensation, as of excitement, tingled through her. She longed to ascertain if the woman was good-looking who made the third in this party of three. She peeped eventually—with the corner of her eye. Lord Bracondale had so placed his guests that he himself faced Theodora, and the lady had her back turned to her.

Thus Theodora's curiosity could not be gratified.

"She is English," she decided; "that round shaped back always is—and very well-bred looking, and not much taste in dress. I wonder if she is old or young—and if that is the husband. Yes, he is unattractive—it must be the husband—and oh, I wonder what they are talking about! Lord Bracondale seems so interested!"

And if she had known it was—

"Really, Monica, how fortunate to have secured you at short notice like this," Lord Bracondale was saying. "I only found I had a free evening at breakfast, and I met Jack on my way to the polo-ground just in the nick of time."

"We love coming," Mrs. Ellerwood replied. "For unsophisticated English people it is a great treat. We go back on Saturday—every one will be asking what is keeping you here so long."

"My plans are vague," Lord Bracondale said, casually. "I might come back any day, or I may stay until well into June—it quite depends upon how amused I am. I rather love Paris."

And to himself he was thinking—

"How I wish that atrocious woman over there with the paradise plume would keep her hat out of the way. Ah, that is better! How lovely she looks to-night! What an exquisite pose of head! And what are those two damned foreigners saying to her, I wonder. Underbred brute, the American, Herryman Hoggenwater! What a name! She is laughing—she evidently finds him amusing. Abominably cattish of the widow not to ask me. I wonder if she has seen me yet. I want to make her bow to me. Ah!" For just then magnetism was too strong for Theodora, and, in spite of her determination, their eyes met.

A thrill, little short of passion, ran through Lord Bracondale as he saw the wild roses flushing her white cheeks—the exquisite flattery to his vanity. Yes, she had seen him, and it already meant something to her.

He raised his champagne glass and sipped a sip, while his eyes, more ardent than they had ever been, sought her face.

And Theodora, for her part, felt a flutter too. She was angry with herself for blushing, such a school-girlish thing to do, Sarah had always told her. She hoped he had not noticed it at that distance—probably not. And what did he mean by drinking her health like that? He—oh, he was—

"Now, truly, Mrs. Brown, you are cruel," Mr. Herryman Hoggenwater said, pathetically, interrupting her thoughts. "I tell you I am simply longing to know if you will come for a drive in my automobile, and you do not answer, but stare into space."

Theodora turned, and then the young American understood that for all her gentle looks it would be wiser not to take this tone with her.

He admired her frantically, he was just "crazy" about her, he told Mrs. McBride later. And so now he exerted himself to please and amuse her with all the vivacity of his brilliant nation.

Theodora was enjoying herself. Environment and atmosphere affected her strongly. The bright pink lights, the sense of night and the soft moon beyond the wide open balcony windows, the scents of flowers, the gayety, and, above all, the knowledge that Lord Bracondale was there, gazing at her whenever opportunity offered, with eyes in which she, unlearned as she was in such things, could read plainly admiration and unrest.

It all went to her head a little, and she became quite animated and full of repartee and sparkle, so that Josiah Brown could hardly believe his eyes and ears when he glanced across at her. This his meek and quiet mouse!

His heart swelled with pride when Mrs. McBride leaned over and said to him:

"You know, Mr. Brown, you have got the most beautiful wife in the world, and I hope you value her properly."

It was this daring quality in his hostess Josiah appreciated so much. "She's not afraid to say anything, 'pon my soul," he said to himself. "I rather think I know my own possession's value!" he answered aloud, with a pompous puffing out of chest, and a cough to clear the throat.

The Austrian Prince on Theodora's right hand pleased her. He had a quiet manner, and the freemasonry of breeding in two people, even of different nations, drew her to talk naturally to him in a friendly way.

He was a fatalist, he told her; what would be would be, and mortals like himself and herself were just scattered leaves, like barks floating down a current where were mostly rocks ahead.

"Then must we strike the rocks whether we wish it or no?" asked Theodora. "Cannot we help ourselves?"

"Ah, madame, for that," he said, "we can strive a little and avoid this one and that, but if it is our fate we will crash against them in the end."

"What a sad philosophy!" said Theodora. "I would rather believe that if one does one's best some kind angel will guide one's bark past the rocks and safely into the smooth waters of the pool beyond."

"You are young," he said, "and I hope you will find it so, but I fear you will have to try very hard, and circumstances may even then be too strong for you."

"In that case I must go under altogether," said Theodora; but her eyes smiled, and that night at least such a possibility seemed far enough away from her.

The Austrian looked across at her husband. Such marriages were rare in his country, and he had thought so too in England. He wondered what their story could be. He wondered how soon she would take a lover—and he realized how infinitely worth while that lover would find his situation.

He wished he were not so old. If she must break up her bark on the rocks, he could take the place of steersman with pleasure. But he was a courteous gentleman and he said none of these things aloud.

Meanwhile, Lord Bracondale was not enjoying his dinner. For the first time for several years he found himself jealous! He, unlike Theodora, knew the meaning of every one of his sensations.

"She is certainly interested in Prince Carolstein," he thought, as he watched her; "he has a European reputation for fascination. She has not looked this way once since the entrées. I wish I could hear what they are talking about. As for that young puppy Hoggenwater, I would like to kick him round the room! Lord, look how he is leaning over her! It sickens me! The young fool!"

Mrs. Ellerwood turned round in her seat and surveyed the room. They had almost come to the end of dinner, and could move their chairs a little. She had the true Englishwoman's feeling when among foreigners—that they were all there as puppets for her entertainment.

"Look, Hector," she said—they were cousins—"did you ever see such a lovely woman as that one over there among the large party, in the black chiffon dress?"

Then Hector committed a *bêtise*.

"Where?" said he, his eyes persistently fixed in another direction.

"There; you can't mistake her, she looks so pure white, and fair, among all these Frenchwomen The one with the blue eyes and the lovely hat with those sweeping feathers. She is exquisitely dressed, and both those men look fearfully devoted to her. Can't you see? Oh, you are stupid!"

"My dear Monica," said Jack Ellerwood, who joined rarely in the conversation, "Hector has been sitting facing this way all through dinner. He is a man who can appreciate what he sees, and I do not fancy has missed much—have you, Hector?" and he smiled a quiet smile.

Mrs. Ellerwood looked at Lord Bracondale and laughed.

"It is I who am stupid," she said. "Naturally you have seen her all the time, and know her probably. Are they cocottes, or Americans, or Russian princesses, or what?—the whole collection?"

"If you mean that large party in the corner, they are most of them friends and acquaintances of mine," he said, rather icily—she had annoyed him—"and they belong to the aristocracies of various nations. Does that satisfy you? I am afraid they are none of them demimondaines, so you will be disappointed this time!"

Mrs. Ellerwood looked at him; she understood now.

"He is in love with the white woman," she thought; "that is why he was so anxious to dine here to-night, when Jack suggested Madrid; that is why he stays in Paris. It is not Esclarmonde de Chartres after all! How excited Aunt Milly will be! I must find out her name."

"She is a beautiful creature," said Jack Ellerwood, as if to himself, while he carefully surveyed Theodora from his position at the side of the table.

Hector Bracondale's irritation rose. Relations were tactless, and he felt sorry he had asked them.

"You must tell me her name, Hector," pleaded Mrs. Ellerwood; "the very white, pretty one I mean."

"Now just to punish your curiosity I shall do no such thing."

"Hector, you are a pig."

"Probably."

"And so selfish."

"Possibly."

"Why mayn't I know? You set a light to all sorts of suspicions."

"Doubly interesting for you, then."

"Provoking wretch!"

"Don't you think you would like some coffee? The waiter is trying to hand you a cup."

Mrs. Ellerwood laughed. She knew there was no use teasing him further; but there were other means, and she must employ them. Theodora had become the pivot upon which some of her world might turn.

The object of this solicitude was quite unconscious of the interest she had created. She did not naturally think she could be of importance to any one. Had she not been the youngest and snubbed always?

The same thought came to her that was conjuring the brain of Lord Bracondale: would there be a chance to speak to-night, or must they each go their way in silence? He meant to assist fate if he could, but having Monica Ellerwood there was a considerable drawback.

Mrs. McBride's party were to take their coffee in one of the *bosquets* outside, and all got up from their table in a few minutes to go out. They would have to pass the *partie à trois*, who were nearer the door. Monica would take her most searching look at them, Lord Bracondale thought; now was the time for action. So as Mrs. McBride came past with Captain Fitzgerald, he rose from his seat and greeted her.

"You have been exceedingly mean," he whispered. "What are you going to do for me to make up for it?"

The widow had a very soft spot in her heart for "Ce beau Bracondale," as she called him, and when he pleaded like that she found him hard to resist.

"Come and see me to-morrow at twelve, and we will talk about it," she said.

"To-morrow!" exclaimed Lord Bracondale; "but I want to talk to her to-night!"

"Get rid of your party, then, and join us for coffee," and the widow smiled archly as she passed on.

Theodora bowed with grave sweetness as she also went by, and most of the others greeted Hector, while one woman stopped and told him she was going to have an automobile party in a day or two, and she hoped he would come.

When they had all gone on Mrs. Ellerwood said:

"I wonder why Americans are so much smarter than we poor English? I can't bear them as a nation though, can you?"

"Yes," said Lord Bracondale. "I think the best friends I have in the world are American. The women particularly are perfectly charming. You feel all the time you are playing a game with really experienced adversaries, and it makes it interesting. They are full of resource, and you know underneath you could never break their hearts. I am not sure if they have any in their own country, but if so they turn into the most wonderful and exquisite bits of mechanism when they come to Europe."

"And you admire that."

"Certainly—hearts are a great bore."

"You were always a cynic, Hector; that is perhaps what makes you so attractive."

"Am I attractive?"

"I can't judge," said Mrs. Ellerwood, nettled for a moment. "I have known you too long, but I hear other women saying so."

"That is comforting, at all events," said Lord Bracondale. "I always have adored women."

"No, you never have, that is just it. You have let them adore you, and utterly spoil you; so now sometimes, Hector, you are insupportable."

"You just said I was attractive."

"I shall not argue further with you," said Mrs. Ellerwood, pettishly.

"And I think we ought to be saying good-night, Hector," interrupted the silent Jack. "We are making an early start for Fontainebleau to-morrow, and Monica likes any amount of sleep."

This did not suit Mrs. Ellerwood at all; but if Jack spoke seldom he spoke to some purpose when he did, and she knew there was no use arguing.

So with a heart full of ungratified curiosity, she at last allowed herself to be packed into Hector's automobile and driven away.

"Of course he'll go and join that other party now, Jack! What *did* you make me come away for, you tiresome thing!" she said to her husband.

"He has done me many a turn in the past," said Jack, laconically.

"Then you think—?"

But Jack refused to think.

V

Theodora was sitting rather on the outskirts of the party in the *bosquet*, her two devoted admirers still on either side of her. All the chairs were arranged informally, and hers was against the opening, so that it proved easy for Lord Bracondale to come up behind her unperceived.

She believed he had gone. She could not see distinctly from where she was, but she had thought she saw the automobile whizzing by. She recognized Mrs. Ellerwood's hat. An unconscious feeling of blankness came over her. She grew more silent.

A lady beyond the Prince spoke to him, and at that moment Mr. Hoggenwater rose to put down her coffee-cup, and in this second of loneliness a deep voice said in her ear:

"I could not go—I wanted to say good-night to you!"

Then Theodora experienced a new emotion; she could not have told herself what it was, but suddenly a gladness spread through her spirit; the moon looked more softly bright, and her sweet eyes dilated and glowed, while that voice, gentle as a dove's, trembled a little as she said:

"Lord Bracondale! Oh, you startled me!"

He drew a chair and sat down behind her.

"How shall we get rid of your Hogginheimer millionaire?" he whispered. "I feel as if I wanted to kill every one who speaks to you to-night."

The half light, the moon, Paris, and the spring-time! Theodora spent the next hour in a dream—a dream of bliss.

Mrs. McBride, with her all-seeing eye, perceived the turn events had taken. She was full of enjoyment herself; she had quite—almost quite—decided to listen to the addresses of Captain Fitzgerald, therefore her heart, not her common-sense, was uppermost this night.

It could not hurt Theodora to have one evening of agreeable conversation, and it would do Herryman Hoggenwater a great deal of good to be obstacled; thus she expressed it to herself. That last success with Princess Waldersheim had turned his empty head. So she called him and planted him in a safe place by an American girl, who would know how to keep him, and then turned to her own affairs again.

The Prince was a man of the world, and understood life. So Theodora and Lord Bracondale were left in peace.

The latter soon moved his chair to a position where he could see her face, rather behind her still, which entailed a slightly leaning over attitude. They were beyond the radius of the lights in the *bosquet*.

Lord Bracondale was perfectly conversant with all moves in the game; he knew how to talk to a woman so that she alone could feel the strength of his devotion, while his demeanor to the world seemed the least compromising.

Theodora had not spoken for a moment after his first speech. It made her heart beat too fast.

"I have been watching you all through dinner," he continued, with only a little pause. "You look immensely beautiful to-night, and those two told you so, I suppose."

"Perhaps they did!" she said. This was her first gentle essay at fencing. She would try to be as the rest were, gay and full of badinage.

"And you liked it?" with resentment.

"Of course I did; you see, I never have heard any of these nice things much. Josiah has always been too ill to go out, and when I was a girl I never saw any people who knew how to say them."

She had turned to look at him as she said this, and his eyes spoke a number of things to her. They were passionate, and resentful, and jealous, and full of something disturbing. Thrills ran through poor Theodora.

His eyes had been capable of looking most of these things before to other women, when he had not meant any of them, but she did not know that.

"Well," he said, "they had better return or recommence their compliments, because I am not in the mood to be polite to them to-night."

"What is your mood?" asked Theodora, and then felt a little frightened at her own daring.

"My mood is one of unrest—I would like to be away alone with you, where we could talk in peace," and he leaned over her so that his lips were fairly close to her ear. "These people jar upon me. I would like to be sitting in the garden at Amalfi, or in a gondola in Venice, and I want to talk about all your beautiful thoughts. You are a new white flower for me, as different as an angel from the other women in the world."

"Am I?" said she, in her tender tones. "I would wish that you should always keep that good thought of me. We shall soon go our different ways. Josiah has decided to leave next week, and we are not likely to meet in England."

"Yes, we are likely to meet—I will arrange it," he said.

There was nothing hesitating about Hector Bracondale—his way with women had always been masterful—and this quality, when mixed with a sudden bending to their desires, was peculiarly attractive. To-night he was drifting—drifting into a current which might carry him beyond his control.

It was now several years since he had been in love even slightly. His position, his appearance, his personal charm, had all combined to spoil a nature capable of great things. Life had always been too smooth. His mother adored him. He had an ample fortune. Every marriageable girl in his world almost had been flung at his head. Women of all classes with one consent had done their best to turn him into a coxcomb and a beast. But he continued to be a man for all that, and went his own way; only as no one can remain stationary, the crust of selfishness and cynicism was perhaps thickening with years, and his soul was growing hidden still deeper beneath it all. From the beginning something in Theodora had spoken to the best in him. He was conscious of feelings of dissatisfaction with himself when he left her, of disgust with the days of unmeaning aims.

He had begun out of idle admiration; he had continued from inclination; but to-night it was *plus fort que lui*, and he knew he was in love.

The habit of indulging any emotion which gave him pleasure was still strong upon him; it was not yet he would begin to analyze where this passion might lead him—might lead them both.

It was too deliciously sweet to sit there and whisper to her sophistries and reasonings, to take her sensitive fancy into new worlds, to play upon her feelings—those feelings which he realized were as fine and as full of tone as the sounds which could be drawn from a Stradivarius violin.

It was a night of new worlds for them both, for if Theodora had never looked into any world at all, he also had never even imagined one which could be so quite divine as this—this shared with her in the moonlight, with the magic of the Tzigane music and the soft spring night.

He had just sufficient mastery over himself left not to overstep the bounds of respectful and deep interest in her. He did not speak a word of love. There was no actual sentence which Theodora felt obliged to resent—and yet through it all was the subtle insinuation that they were more than friends—or would be more than friends.

And when it was all over, and Theodora's pulses were calmer as she lay alone on her pillow, she had a sudden thrill of fear. But she put it aside—it was not her nature to think herself the object of passions. "I would be a very silly woman to flatter myself so," she said to herself, and then she went to sleep.

Lord Bracondale stayed awake for hours, but he did not sup with Esclarmonde de Chartres or Marion de Beauvoison. And the Café de Paris—and Maxims—and the afterwards—saw him no more.

Once again these houris asked each other, "Mais qu'est-ce qu'il a! Ce bel Hector? Oú se cache-t-il?"

VI

Before she went to bed in her hotel in the Rue de Rivoli, Monica Ellerwood wrote to her aunt.

PARIS, *May 15th.*

"MY DEAR AUNT MILLY,—We have had a delicious little week, Jack and I, quite like an old honeymoon pair—and to-day we ran across Hector, who has remained hidden until now. He is looking splendid, just as handsome and full of life as ever, so it does not tell upon his constitution, that is one mercy! Not like poor Ernest Bretherton, who, if you remember, was quite broken up by her last year. And I have one good piece of news for you, dear Aunt Milly. I do not believe he is so frantically wrapped up in this Esclarmonde de Chartres woman after all—in spite of that diamond chain at Monte Carlo. For to-night he took us to dine at Armenonville—although Jack particularly wanted to go to the Madrid—and when we got there we saw at once why! There was a most beautiful woman dining there with a party, and Hector never took his eyes off her the whole of dinner, Jack says—I had my back that way—and he got rid of us as soon as he could and went and joined them. Very young she looked, but I suppose married, from her pearls and clothes—American probably, as she was perhaps too well dressed for one of us; but quite a lady and awfully pretty. Hector was so snappish about it, and would not tell her name, that it makes me sure he is very much in love with her, and Jack thinks so too. So, dear Aunt Milly, you need have no more anxieties about him, as she can't have been married long, she looks so young, and so must be quite safe. Jack says Hector is thoroughly able to take care of himself, anyway, but I know how all these things worry you. If I can find out her name before I go I will, though perhaps you think it is out of the frying-pan into the fire, as it makes him no more in the mood to marry Morella Winmarleigh than before. Unless, of course, this new one is unkind to him. We shall be home on Saturday, dear Aunt Milly, and I will come round to lunch on Sunday and give you all my news.

"Your affectionate niece,

"MONICA ELLERWOOD".

Which epistle jarred upon Hector's mother when she read it over coffee at her solitary dinner on the following night.

"Poor dear Monica!" she said to herself. "I wonder where she got this strain from—her father's family, I suppose—I wish she would not be so—bald."

Then she sat down and wrote to her son—she was not even going to the opera that night. And if she had looked up in the tall mirror opposite, she would have seen a beautiful, stately lady with a puckered, plaintive frown on her face.

If a woman absolutely worships a man, even if she is only his mother, she is bound to spend many moments of unhappiness, and Lady Bracondale was no exception to the general rule. Hector had always gone his own way, and there were several aspects of his life she disapproved of. These visits to Paris—his antipathy to matrimony—his boredom with girls—such nice girls she knew, too, and had often thrown him with!—his delight in big-game shooting in alarming and impossible countries—and, above all, his absolute indifference to Morella Winmarleigh, the only woman who really and truly in her heart of hearts Lady Bracondale thought worthy of him, although she would have accepted several other girls as choosing the lesser evil to bachelorhood. But Morella Winmarleigh was perfection! She owned the enormous property adjoining Bracondale; she was twenty-six years old, of unblemished reputation, nice looking, and not—not one of those modern women who are bound to cause anxieties. Under any circumstances one could count upon Morella Winmarleigh behaving with absolute propriety. A girl born to be a mother-in-law's joy.

But Hector persistently remained at large. It was not that he openly defied his mother—he simply made love to her whenever they were together, twisted her round his finger, and was off again.

"To see mother with Hector," Lady Annigford said, "is a wonderful sight. Although I adore him myself, I am not at the stage she is! She sits there beaming on him exactly like an exceedingly proud and fond cat with new kittens. He treats her as if she were a young and beautiful woman, caresses her, pets her, pays not the least attention to anything she says, and does absolutely what he pleases!"

Hector and Lady Bracondale together had often made the women who were in love with him jealous.

When she had finished her letter the stately lady read it over carefully—she had a certain tact, and Hector must be cajoled to return, not irritated.

Monica's epistle, in spite of that touch of vulgarity which she had deplored, had held out some grains of comfort. She had been getting really anxious over this affair with the—French person. Even to herself Lady Bracondale would not use any of the terms which usually designate ladies of the type of Esclarmonde de Chartres.

Since her brother-in-law Evermond had returned from Monte Carlo bringing that disturbing story of the diamond chain, she had been on thorns—of such a light mind and always so full of worldly gossip, Evermond!

Hector had gone from Monte Carlo to Venice, and then to Paris, where he had been for more than a month, and she had heard that men could become quite infatuated and absolutely ruined by these creatures. So for him to have taken a fancy to a married American was considerably better than that. She had met several members of this nation herself in England, and were they not always very discreet, with well-balanced heads! So altogether the puckered frown soon left her smooth brow, and she was able to resume the knitting of a tie she was doing for her son, with a spirit more or less at rest, though she sighed now and then as she remembered Morella Winmarleigh could not be expected to wait forever—and her cherished vision of perfectly behaved, vigorously healthy grandchildren was still a long way from being realized. For with such a mother what perfect children they would be! This was always her final reflection.

VII

At twelve o'clock punctually Lord Bracondale was ushered into Mrs. McBride's sitting-room at the Ritz, the day after her dinner-party at Armenonville. He expected she would not be ready to receive him for at least half an hour; having said twelve he might have known she meant half-past, but he was in a mood of impatience, and felt obliged to be punctual.

He was suffering more or less from a reaction. He had begun towards morning to realize the manner in which he had spent the evening was not altogether wise. Not that he had the least intention of not repeating his folly—indeed, he was where he was at this hour for no other purpose than to enlist the widow's sympathy, and her co-operation in arranging as many opportunities for similar evenings as together they could devise.

After all, she only kept him waiting twenty minutes, and he had been rather amused looking at the piles of bric-à-brac obsequious art dealers had left for this rich lady's inspection.

A number of spurious bronzes warranted pure antique, clocks, brocades, what not, lying about on all the available space.

"And I wonder what it will look like in her marble palace halls," he thought, as he passed from one article to another.

"I am just too sorry to keep you, mon cher Bracondale," Mrs. McBride said, presently, suddenly opening the adjoining door a few inches, "but it is a quite exasperating hat which has delayed me. I can't get the thing on at the angle I want. I—"

"Mayn't I come and help, dear lady?" interrupted Hector. "I know all about the subject. I had to buy forty-seven at Monte Carlo, and see them all tried on, too—and only lately! Do ask Marie to open that door a little wider; I will decide in a minute how it should be."

"Insolent!" said the widow, who spoke French with perfect fluency and a quite marvellously pure American accent. But she permitted the giggling and beaming Marie to open the door wide, and let Hector advance and kiss her hand.

He then took a chair by the dressing-table and inspected the situation.

Seven or eight dainty bandboxes strewed the floor, some of their contents peeping from them—feathers, aigrettes, flowers, impossible birds—all had their place, and on the sofa were three *chef d'œuvres* ruthlessly tossed aside. While in the widow's fair hands was a gem of gray tulle and the most expensive feather heart of woman could desire.

"You see," she said, plaintively, "it is meant to go just so," and she placed it once more upon her head, a handsome head of forty-five, fresh and well preserved and comely. "But the vile-tempered thing refuses to stay there once I let go, and no pin will correct it."

"Base ingratitude," said Lord Bracondale, with feeling; "but couldn't you stuff these in the hiatus," and he tenderly lifted a bunch of nut-brown curls from the dressing-table. "They would fill up the gap and keep the fractious thing steady."

"Of course they would," said Mrs. McBride; "but I have a rooted objection to auxiliary nature trimmings. That bunch was sent with the hat, and Marie has been trying to persuade me to wear it ever since we began this struggle. But I won't! My hair's my own, and I don't mean to have any one else's alongside of it. There is my trouble."

"If milor were to hold madame's 'at one side, while I de other, madame might force her emerald parrot pin through him," suggested Marie, which advice was followed, and the widow beamed with satisfaction at the gratifying result.

"There!" she exclaimed, with a sigh of relief, "that will do; and I am just ready. Gloves, handkerchief—oh! and my purse, Marie." And in five minutes more she was leading the way back into her sitting-room.

"I have not ordered lunch until one o'clock," she said, "so we have oceans of time to talk and tell each other secrets. Sit down, jeune homme, and confess to me." She pointed to a *bergère*, but it was filled with Italian embroideries. "Marie, take this rubbish away!" she called, and presently some chairs were made clear.

"And what must I confess?" asked Hector, when they were seated. "That I am frantically in love with you, and your coldness is driving me wild?"

"Certainly not!" said the widow, while she rose again and began to arrange some giant roses in a wonderful basket which looked as if it had just arrived—her shrewd eye had seen the card, "From Captain Fitzgerald, with his best bonjour." "Certainly not! We are going to talk truth, or, to punish you, I shall not ask you to meet her again, and I shall warn her father of your strictly dishonorable intentions."

"You would not be so cruel!"

"Yes I would. And it is what I ought to do, anyway. She is as innocent as a woolly lamb, and unsophisticated and guileless, and will probably be falling in love with you. You take the wind out of the sails of that husband of hers, you see!"

"Do I?" said Hector, with overdone incredulity.

She looked at him. His long, lithe limbs stretched out, every line indicative of breeding and strength. She noted the shape of his head, the perfect grooming, his lazy, insolent grace, his whimsical smile. Englishmen of this class were certainly the most provokingly beautiful creatures in the world.

"It is because they have done nothing but order men, kill beasts, and subjugate women for generations," she said to herself. "Lazy, naughty darlings! If they came to our country and worked their brains a little, they would soon lose that look. But it would be a pity," she added—"yes, a pity."

"What are you thinking of?" asked Lord Bracondale, while she gazed at him.

"I was thinking you are a beautiful, useless creature. Just like all your nation. You think the world is made for you; in any case, all the women and animals to kill are."

"What an abominable libel! But I am fond of both things—women and animals to kill."

"And you class them equally—or perhaps the animals are ahead."

"Indeed not always," said Hector, reassuringly. "Some women have quite the first place."

"You are too flattering!" retorted the widow. "Those sentiments are all very well for your own poor-spirited, down-trodden women, but they won't do for Americans! A man has to learn a number of lessons before he is fitted to cope with them."

"Oh, tell me," said Hector.

"He has got to learn to wait, for one thing, to wait about for hours if necessary, and not to lose his temper, because the woman can't make up her mind to be in time for things, or to change it often as to where she will dine. Then he has to learn to give up any pleasure of his own for hers—and travel when she wants to travel, or stay home when she wants to go alone. If he is an Englishman he don't have brains enough to make the money, but he must let her spend what he has got how she likes, and not interfere with her own."

"And in return he gets?"

"The woman he happens to want, I suppose." And the widow laughed, showing her wonderfully preserved brilliant white teeth.

"You enunciate great truths, belle dame!" said Hector, "and your last sentence is the greatest of all—'*The woman he happens to want.*'"

"Which brings us back to our muttons—in this case only a defenceless baby lamb. Now tell me what you are here for, trying to cajole me with your good looks and mock humility."

"I am here to ask you to help me to see her again, then," said Hector, who knew when to be direct. "I have only met her three times, as you know, but I have fallen in love, and she is going away next week, and there is only one Paris in the world."

"You can do a great deal of mischief in a week," Mrs. McBride said, looking at him again critically. "I ought not to help you, but I can't resist you—there! What can we devise?"

It is possible the probability of Theodora's father making a fourth may have had something thing to do with her complaisance. Anyway, it was decided that if feasible the four should spend a day at Versailles.

They should go in their two automobiles in time for breakfast at the Réservoirs. They would start, Theodora in Mrs. McBride's with her, and Captain Fitzgerald with Lord Bracondale, and each couple could spend the afternoon as they pleased, dining again at the Réservoirs and whirling back to Paris in the moonlight. A truly rural and refreshing programme, good for the soul of man.

"And I can rely upon you to get rid of the husband?" said Lord Bracondale, finally. "I do not see the poetry of the affair with his bald head and mutton-chop whiskers as an accessory."

"Leave that to Captain Fitzgerald and myself," Mrs. McBride said, proudly. "I have a scheme that Mr. Brown shall spend the day with Clutterbuck R. Tubbs, examining some new machinery they are both interested in. Leave it to me!" The part of *Deus ex machina* was always a rôle the widow loved.

Then they descended to an agreeable lunch in the restaurant, with a numerous party of her friends as usual, and Lord Bracondale felt afterwards full of joy and hope, to continue his sinful path unrepenting.

The days that intervened before Theodora saw him again were uneventful and full of blankness. The walks in the Bois appeared more tedious than ever in the morning, the drives in the Acacias more exasperating. It was a continual alertness to see if she caught sight of a familiar face, but she never did. Fate was against them, as she sometimes is when she means to compensate soon after by some glorious day of the gods. And although Lord Bracondale called at her hotel and walked where he thought he should see her, and even drove in the Acacias, they had no meeting.

Josiah did not feel himself sufficiently strong to stand the air of theatres, and they went nowhere in the evenings. He was keeping himself for his own dinner-party, which was to take place at the Madrid on the Monday.

Captain Fitzgerald had arranged it, and besides Mrs. McBride several of his friends were coming, and a special band of wonderfully talented Tziganes, who were delighting Paris that year, had been engaged to play to them. If only the weather should remain fine all would be well.

A surprise awaited Theodora on Saturday morning. A friendly note from Mrs. McBride arrived, asking her if she would spend the day with her at Versailles, as she had asked her husband to do her a favor and lunch with Mr. Clutterbuck R. Tubbs.

Theodora awaited Josiah's presence at the *premier déjeuner*, which they took in their salon, with absolute excitement. He came in, a pompous smile on his face.

"Good-day, my love," he said, blandly. "That charming widow writes me this morning, asking if I will do her a favor, and take her friend, Mr. Clutterbuck Tubbs, to examine that machinery for the separation of fats we both have an interest in, and he suggests I should lunch with him, as he is very anxious to have my opinion upon the merits of it."

"Yes," said Theodora.

"She also says," referring to the letter in his hand, "she will take charge of you for the day, and take you to Versailles, which I know you wish to go to. She wants an answer at once, as she will call for you at twelve o'clock if we accept."

"I have heard from her, too," said Theodora. "What shall you answer, Josiah?" and she looked out of the window.

"Oh, I may as well go, I think. There is money in the invention, or that old gimlet-eye would not be so keen about it; I talked the matter over with him at Armenonville the other night."

"Then shall you write or shall I?" said Theodora, as evenly as she could. "Her servant is waiting."

VIII

Theodora hummed to herself a glad little *chansonnette* as she changed her breakfast negligee for the freshest and loveliest of her spring frocks. She did not know why she was so happy. There had been no word of any one else being of the party, only she and Mrs. McBride, but Versailles would be exquisite on such a day, and something whispered to her that she might not yawn.

The most radiant vision awaited the widow, when, with unusual punctuality, her automobile stopped at the hotel door. She came in. She was voluble, she flattered Josiah. So good of him to take Mr. Tubbs—and she hoped it would not tire him. Theodora should be well looked after. They might be late and even dine at Versailles, she said, and Mr. Brown was not to be anxious—*she* would be responsible for the safe return of his beautiful little wife. (Theodora was five foot seven at least, but her small head and extreme slenderness gave people the feeling she was little—something to be protected and guarded always.)

Josiah was affable. Mrs. McBride's words were so smooth and so many, he had no time to feel Theodora was going to dine out without him, or that anything had been arranged for ultimate ends.

The automobile had almost reached Suresnes before the widow said to her guest:

"Your father and Lord Bracondale have promised to meet us at the Réservoirs. Captain Fitzgerald told me how you wanted to go to Versailles, and how your husband is not strong enough to take these excursions, so I thought we might have this little day out there, while he is engaged with Mr. Clutterbuck Tubbs."

"How sweet of you!" said Theodora.

As they rushed through the smiling country, both women's spirits rose, and Mrs. McBride's were the spirits of experience and did not mount without due cause. Since she had been a girl in Dakota and passionately in love with her first husband—the defunct McBride was a second venture—she had not met a man who could quicken her pulse like Captain Fitzgerald. It was a curious coincidence that they both had already two partners to regret. It was an extra link between them, and Jane McBride, who was superstitious, read the omen to mean that this time each had met his true mate.

"If he is irresistible to-day, I think I shall clinch matters," she was saying to herself.

While Theodora's musings ran:

"How beautiful Versailles will look, and I dare say he will know all about its history, and be able to tell me interesting things; and oh! I am so glad I put on this frock, and oh! I am so happy."

And aloud they spoke of paradise plumes and the new gray, and the merits and demerits of Callot and Doucet and Jeanne Valez. And the widow said some bright American things about husbands and the world in general that conveyed crisp truths.

The drive seemed all too short, and there were their two cavaliers in the court-yard awaiting them at the Réservoirs, having arrived just before them.

To the end of her life Theodora will remember that glorious May day. Its even minutest detail, the color of the chestnut-trees, the tint of the sky, the scent in the air, every line of his figure and turn of his head, every look in his eyes—and they were many and varied—and also and alas! every growing emotion in her own heart. But at the moment all was gladness, and exquisite, young, irresponsible joy. *Sans arrière-pensée* or disquieting reflection.

She wondered which of the two men was the handsomer as she got out of the automobile—dear, darling papa or Lord Bracondale; both were quite show creatures of their age, and both were of the same class and knowledge of *savoir-vivre*. Every one said such polite and gracious things, it was all so smooth and gay, and it seemed so natural that they should take a turn up towards the château while breakfast was being prepared.

Half-past one o'clock was time enough to eat, the widow said.

"I want to show you a number of spots I love," Hector announced, choosing a different path to the other pair. "And it is a day we can be happy in, can't we?"

"I want to be happy," said Theodora.

"Then we shall go no farther now; we shall sit on this seat and admire the view. See, we are quite alone and undisturbed; all the world has gone home to breakfast."

Then he looked at her, and though he really did try at this stage to be reasonable, something of the intense attraction he felt for her blazed in his eyes.

She was sufficiently delectable a picture to turn the sagest head. There was something so absolutely pure white about that skin, it seemed good to eat, flawless, unlined, unblemished, under this brilliant light.

The way her silvery blond hair grew was just the right way a woman's hair ought to grow, he thought; low on a high, broad brow, rippling and soft, and quantities of it. What could it be like to caress it, to run one's fingers through it, to bury one's face in it? Ah! and then there were her tender eyes, dewy and shadowed with dark lashes, and so intensely blue. His glance wandered farther afield. Such a figure! slender and graceful and fine. There was something almost childish about it all; the innocent look of a very young girl, with the polish of the woman, garbed by an artist. It seemed the great pearls in her ears were not more milkily white than her throat, and he was sure were also her little slender hands, that did not fidget, but lay idly in her lap, holding her blue parasol. He would like to have taken off her gloves to see.

Passionate devotion was surging up in his breast.

And he was an Englishman, and it was still the morning. There was no moon now and he had not even breakfasted! This shows sufficiently to what state he had come.

"I want you to tell me all about Versailles," she said, looking to the left and the gray wing beyond the chapel. "Its histories and its meanings. I used to read about it all after Sarah brought me here once for our treat, but you probably are learned upon the subject, and I want to know."

"I would much rather hear what you did when Sarah brought you here for your treat," he said.

"Oh! it was a very simple day," and she leaned back and laughed softly at the recollection. "Papa was very hard up at that time, you know, and we were rather poor, so we came as cheaply as we could, Sarah, Clementine, and I, and I remember there were some very snuffy men in the train—we could not go first-class, you see—and one of them rather frightened me."

"The brute!" said Hector.

"I think I was about fourteen."

"And even then perfectly beautiful, I expect," he commented to himself.

"We walked up from the station, and oh! we saw all the galleries and we ran all over the park, but we missed the way to Trianon somehow and never saw that, and when we got back here we were too tired to start again. We had only had sandwiches, you see, that we brought with us, and some funny little drinks at a café down there," and she pointed vaguely towards the lake, "because we found we had only one franc fifty between us all. But we were so happy, and Clementine knows a great deal, and told us many things which were quite different from what was in the guide-books—but it seems so long, long ago. Do you know it must be six years." And she looked at him seriously.

"Half a lifetime!" agreed Hector, with a whimsical smile.

"Oh! you are laughing at me!" she said, and there was a cloud in the blue stars which looked up at him.

He made a movement nearer her—while his deep voice took every tone of tenderness.

"Indeed, indeed I am not—you dear little girl! I love to hear of your day. I was only smiling to think that six years ago you were a baby child, and I was then an old man in feeling—let me see, I was twenty-five, and I was in Russia."

He stopped suddenly; there were some circumstances which, sitting there beside her, he would rather not remember connected with Russia.

This was one of the peculiarities of Theodora. There was something about her which seemed to wither up all low or vicious things. It was not that she filled people with ascetic thoughts of saints and angels and their mother in heaven, only she seemed suddenly to enhance simple joys with beauty and charm.

They talked on for half an hour, and with every moment he discovered fresh qualities of sweetness and light in her gentle heart.

She was not ill educated either, but she had never speculated upon things, she took them for granted just as they were, and *Jean d'Agrève* was probably the only awakening book she had ever read.

Hector all at once seemed to realize his mother's vision, and to understand for the first time what marriage might mean. That to possess this exquisite bit of God's finished work for his very own, to live with her in the country, at old Bracondale, to see her honored and adored, surrounded by little children—his children—would be a dream of bliss far, far beyond any dream he had ever known. A domestic, tender dream of sweetness that he had always laughed at before as a final thing when life's other joys should be over, and now it seemed suddenly to be the only heaven and completion of his soul's desire.

Then he remembered Josiah Brown with a hideous pang of pain and bitterness—and they went in to lunch.

Theodora was so gay! Captain Fitzgerald and Mrs. McBride were already seated when they joined them in the restaurant. Most of the other visitors had finished—it was almost two o'clock.

There was a good deal of black middle in the widow's eyes, Theodora noticed, and wondered to herself if she had had a happy and exciting hour too. Papa looked complacent and handsomer than ever, she thought. She did hope it was going well. And she wondered how they were to dispose of their afternoon.

The widow soon settled this. She had, she said, a wild desire to rush through the air for a little—she *must* have her chauffeur go at full speed—somewhere—anywhere—her nerves needed calming! And Captain Fitzgerald had agreed to accompany her. Their destination was unknown, and they might not be back for tea, so Lord Bracondale must take the greatest care of Theodora and give her some if they did not turn up. They certainly would for dinner, but eight o'clock would be time enough for that.

When your destination is unknown you can never say how many hours it will take to get there and back, she pointed out. And no one felt inclined to argue with her about this obvious truth!

Now if Theodora had been a free unmarried girl, or a freer widow, it is highly probable fate would not have arranged this long afternoon in blissful surroundings undisturbed by any one. As it was, who knows if the goddess settled it with a smile on her lip or a tear in her eye? It was settled, at all events, and looked as if it were going to contain some moments worth remembering.

IX

"And what is your pleasure, fair queen?" Hector said, as they listened to the diminishing noise of the widow's Mercédès. "We are alone, and we have the world before us. Issue your commands."

"No," said Theodora, and she pouted her red lips. "I want you to settle that. I want you to arrange for whatever you think would give me the greatest pleasure. Then I shall know if you understand me and guess what I would like."

This was the most daring speech she had ever made, and she was surprised at her own temerity.

"Very well," he said. "That means you belong to me until they return," and a thrill ran through him. "Has not your father, has not your hostess, given you into my charge? And, now you yourself have sealed the compact, we shall see if I can make you happy."

As he said the words "you belong to me," Theodora thrilled too—a sensation as of an electric shock almost quivered through her. Belonged to him—ah!—what would that mean?

He called his chauffeur, who started the automobile and drove under the covered *porte cochère* where they stood.

Lord Bracondale had not spoken all the time he was helping her in and arranging rugs with the tenderest solicitude, but when they were settled and started—it was a coupé with a great deal of glass about it, so that they got plenty of air—he turned to her.

"Now, do you know what I am going to do with you, madame? I shall only unfold my plans bit by bit, and watch your face to see if I have chosen well. I am going to take you first to the Petit Trianon, and we are going to walk leisurely through the rooms. I am not going to worry you with much sight-seeing and tourists and lessons of history, but I want you to glance at this setting of the life picture of poor Marie Antoinette, because it is full of sentiment and it will make you appreciate more the *hameau* and her playground afterwards. Something tells me you would rather see these things than all the fine pictures and salons of the stiff château."

"Oh yes," said Theodora; "you have guessed well this time."

"Then here we are, almost arrived," he said, presently.

They had been going very fast, and could see the square, white house in front of them, and when they alighted at the gates she found the guardian was an old friend of Lord Bracondale's, and they were left free to wander alone in the rooms between the batches of tourists.

But every one knows the Petit Trianon, and can surmise how its beauties appealed to Theodora.

"Oh, the poor, poor queen!" she said, with a sad ring in her expressive voice, when they came to the large salon; "and she sat here and played on her harpsichord—and I wonder if she and Fersen were ever alone—and I wonder if she really loved him—"

Then she stopped suddenly; she had told herself she must never talk about love to any one. It was a subject that she must have nothing to do with. It could never come her way, now she was married to Josiah Brown, and it would be unwise to discuss it, even in the abstract.

The same beautiful, wild-rose tint tinged the white velvet as once before when she had spoken of *Jean d'Agrève*, and again Lord Bracondale experienced a sensation of satisfaction.

But this time he would not let her talk about the weather. The subject of love interested him, too.

"Yes, I am sure she did," he said, "and I always shall believe Fersen was her lover; no life, even a queen's, can escape one love."

"I suppose not," said Theodora, very low, and she looked out of the window.

"Love is not a passion which asks our leave if he may come or no, you see," Hector continued, trying to control his voice to sound dispassionate and discursive—he knew he must not frighten her. "Love comes in a thousand unknown, undreamed-of ways. And then he gilds the world and makes it into heaven."

"Does he?" almost whispered Theodora.

"And think what it must have been to a queen, married to a tiresome, unattractive Bourbon—and Fersen was young and gallant and thoughtful for her slightest good, and, from what one hears and has read, he must have understood her, and been her friend as well—and sometimes she must have forgotten about being a queen for a few moments—in his arms—"

Theodora drew a long, long breath, but she did not speak.

"And perhaps, if we knew, the remembrance of those moments may have been her glory and consolation in the last dark hours."

"Oh! I hope so!" said Theodora.

Then she walked on quickly into the quaint, little, low-ceilinged bedroom. Oh, she must get out into the air—or she must talk of furniture, or curtain stuffs, or where the bath had been!

Love, love, love! And did it mean life after all?—since even this far-off love of this poor dead queen had such power to move her. And perhaps Fersen was like—but this last thought caused her heart to beat too wildly.

There were no roses now, she was very pale as she said: "It saddens me, this. Let us go out into the sun."

They descended the staircase again almost in silence, and on through the little door in the court-yard wall into the beautiful garden beyond.

"Show me where she was happy, where you know she was happy before any troubles came. I want to be gay again," said Theodora.

So they walked down the path towards the *hameau*.

"What have I done?" Lord Bracondale wondered. "Her adorable face went quite white. Her soul is no longer the open book I have found it. There are depths and depths, but I must fathom them all."

"Oh, how I love the spring-time!" exclaimed Theodora, and her voice was full of relief. "Look at those greens, so tender and young, and that peep of the sky! Oh, and those dear, pretty little dolls' houses! Let us hasten; I want to go and play there, and make butter, too! Don't you?"

"Ah, this is good," he said; "and I want just what you want."

Her face was all sweet and joyous as she turned it to him.

"Let's pretend we lived then," she said, "and I am the miller's daughter of this dear little mill, and you are the bailiff's son who lives opposite, and you have come with your corn to be ground. Oh, and I shall make a bargain, and charge you dear!" and she laughed and swung her parasol back, while the sun glorified her hair into burnished silver.

"What bargain could you make that I would not agree to willingly?" he asked.

"Perhaps some day I shall make one with you—or want to—that you will not like," she said, "and then I shall remind you of this day and your gallant speech."

"And I shall say then as I say now. I will make any bargain with you, so long as it is a bargain which benefits us both."

"Ah, you are a Normand, you hedge!" she laughed, but he was serious.

They walked all around the *laiterie*, and all the time she was gay and whimsical, and to herself she was saying, "I am unutterably happy, but we must not talk of love."

"Now you have had enough of this," Lord Bracondale said, when they were again in view of the house, "and I am going to take you into a forest like the babes in the woods, and we shall go and lose ourselves and forget the world altogether. The very sight of these harmless tourists in the distance jars upon me to-day. I want you alone and no one else. Come."

And she went.

"I have never been here before," said Theodora, as they turned into the Forest of Marly. "And you have been wise in your choice so far. I love trees."

"You see how I study and care for the things which belong to me," said Hector. It gave him ridiculous pleasure to announce that sentence again—ridiculous, unwarrantable pleasure.

Theodora turned her head away a little. She would like to have continued the subject, but she did not dare.

Presently they came to a side *allée*, and after going up it about a mile the automobile stopped, and they got out and walked down a green glade to the right.

Oh, and I wonder if any of you who read know the Forest of Marly, and this one green glade that leads down to the centre of a star where five avenues meet? It is all soft grass and splendid trees, and may have been a *rendezvous de chasse* in the good old days, when life—for the great—was fair in France.

It is very lonely now, and if you want to spend some hours in peace you can almost count upon solitude there.

"Now, is not this beautiful?" he asked her, as they neared the centre, "and soon you will see why I carry this rug over my arm. I am going to take you right to the middle of the star until you see five paths for you to choose from, all green and full of glancing sunlight, and when you have selected one we will penetrate down it and sit under a tree. Is it good—my idea?"

"Very good," said Theodora. Then she was silent until they reached the *rond-point*.

There was that wonderful sense of aloofness and silence—hardly even the noise of a bird. Only the green, green trees, and here and there a shaft of sunlight turning them into the shade of a lizard's back.

An ideal spot for—poets and dreamers—and lovers—Theodora thought.

"Now we are here! Look this way and that! Five paths for us to choose from!"

Then something made Theodora say, "Oh, let us stay in the centre, in this one round place, where we can see them all and their possibilities."

"And do you think uncertain possibilities are more agreeable perhaps than certain ends?" he asked.

"I never speculate," said Theodora.

"As you will, then," he said, while he looked into her eyes, and he placed the rug up against a giant tree between two avenues, so that their view really only extended down three others now.

"We have turned our backs on the road we came," he said, "and on another road that leads in a roundabout way to the Grande Avenue again. So now we must look into the unknown and the future."

"It seems all very green and fair," said Theodora, and she leaned back against the tree and half closed her eyes.

He lay on the grass at her feet, his hat thrown off beside him, and in a desert island they could not have been more alone and undisturbed.

The greatest temptation that Hector Bracondale had ever yet had in his life came to him then. To make love to her, to tell her of all the new thoughts she had planted in his soul, of the windows she had opened wide to the sunlight. To tell her that he loved her, that he longed to touch even the tips of her fingers, that the thought of caressing her lips and her eyes and her hair drove the blood coursing madly through his veins. That to dream of what life could be like, if she were really his own, was a dream of intoxicating bliss.

And something of all this gleamed in his eyes as he gazed up at her—and Theodora, all unused to the turbulence of emotion, was troubled and moved and yet wildly happy. She looked away down the centre avenue, and she began to speak fast with a little catch in her breath, and Hector clinched his hands together and gazed at a beetle in the grass, or otherwise he would have taken her in his arms.

"Tell me the story of all these avenues," she said; "tell me a fairy story suitable to the day."

And he fell in with her mood. So he began:

"Once Upon a Time There Was a Fairy Prince and Princess."

"Once upon a time there was a fairy prince and princess, and a witch had enchanted them and put them in a green forest, but had set a watch-dog over Love—so that the poor Cupid with his bow and arrows might not shoot at them, and they were told they might live and enjoy the green wood and find what they could of sport and joy. But Cupid laughed. 'As if,' he said, 'there is anything in a green wood of good without me—and my shafts!' So while the watch-dog slept—it was a warm, warm day in May, just such as this—he shot an arrow at the prince and it entered his heart. Then he ran off laughing.

'That is enough for one day,' he said. And the poor prince suffered and suffered because he was wounded and the princess had not received a dart, too—and could not feel for him."

"Was she not even sympathetic?" asked Theodora, and again there was that catch in her breath.

"Yes, she was sympathetic," he continued, "but this was not enough for the prince; he wanted her to be wounded, too."

"How very, very cruel of him," said Theodora.

"But men are cruel, and the prince was only a man, you know, although he was in a green forest with a lovely princess."

"And what happened?" asked Theodora.

"Well, the watch-dog slept on, so that a friendly zephyr could come, and it whispered to the prince: 'At the end of all these allées, which lead into the future, there is only one thing, and that is Love; he bars their gates. As soon as you start down one, no matter which, you will find him, and when he sees your princess he will shoot an arrow at her, too.'"

"Oh, then the princess of course never went down an allée," said Theodora—and she smiled radiantly to hide how her heart was beating—"did she?"

"The end of the story I do not know," said Lord Bracondale; "the fairy who told it to me would not say what happened to them, only that the prince was wounded, deeply wounded, with Love's arrow. Aren't you sorry for the prince, beautiful princess?"

Theodora opened her blue parasol, although no ray of sunshine fell upon her there. She was going through the first moment of this sort in her life. She was quite unaccustomed to fencing, or to any intercourse with men—especially men of his world. She understood this story had himself and herself for hero and heroine; she felt she must continue the badinage—anything to keep the tone as light as it could be, with all these new emotions flooding her being and making her heart beat. It was almost pain she experienced, the sensation was so intense, and Hector read of these things in her eyes and was content. So he let his voice grow softer still, and almost whispered again:

"And aren't you sorry for the prince—beautiful princess?"

"I am sorry for any one who suffers," said Theodora, gently, "even in a fairy story."

And as he looked at her he thought to himself, here was a rare thing, a beautiful woman with a tender heart. He knew she would be gentle and kind to the meanest of God's creatures. And again the vision of her at Bracondale came to him—his mother would grow to love her perhaps even more than Morella Winmarleigh! How she would glorify everything commonplace with those tender ways of hers! To look at her was like looking up into the vast, pure sky, with the light of heaven beyond. And yet he lay on the grass at her feet with his mind full of thoughts and plans and desires to drag this angel down from her high heaven—into his arms!

Because he was a man, you see, and the time of his awakening was not yet.

X

Man is a hunter—a hunter always. He may be a poor thing and hunt only a few puny aims, or he may be a strong man and choose big game. But he is hunting, hunting—something—always.

And primitive life seems like the spectrum of light—composed of three primary colors, and white and black at the beginning and ending of it. And the three colors of blue, red, and yellow have their counterparts in the three great passions in man—to hunt his food, to continue his species, and to kill his enemy.

And white and black seem like birth and death—and there is the sun, which is the soul and makes the colors, and allows of all combinations and graduations of beautiful other shades from them for parallels to all other qualities and instincts, only the original are those great primary forces—to hunt his food, to continue his species, and to kill his enemy.

And if this is so to the end of time, man will be the same, I suppose, until civilization has emasculated the whole of nature and so ends the world! Or until this wonderful new scientist has perfected his researches to the point of creating human life by chemical process, as well as his present discovery of animating jellyfish!

Who knows? But by that time it will not matter to any of us!

Meanwhile, man is at the stage that when he loves a woman he wishes to possess her, and, in a modified form, he wishes to steal her, if necessary, from another, or kill the enemy who steals her from him.

But the Sun of the Soul is there, too, so the poor old world is not in such a very bad case after all.

And how the *bon Dieu* must smile sadly to Himself when He looks down on priests and nuns and hermits and fanatics, and sees how they have distorted His beautiful scheme of things with their narrow ideas. Trying to eliminate the red out of His spectrum, instead of ennobling and glorifying it all with the Sun of the Soul.

And all of you who are great reasoners and arguers will laugh at this ridiculous little simile of life drawn by a woman; but I do not care. I have had my outburst, and said what I wanted to. So now we can get back to the two—who were not yet lovers—under their green tree in the Forest of Marly.

"But you must be able to guess the end," Theodora was saying; "and oh, I want to know, if all the roads were barred by love—how did they get out of the wood?"

"They took him with them," said Lord Bracondale, and he touched the edge of her dress gently with a wild flower he had picked in the grass, while into his eyes crept all the passion he felt and into his voice all the tenderness.

Now if Theodora had ever read *La Faute de L'Abbé Mouret* she would have known just what proximity and the spring-time was doing for them both.

But she had not read, and did not know. All she was conscious of was a wild thrilling of her pulses, an extraordinary magnetic force that seemed to draw her—draw her nearer—nearer to what? Even that she did not know or ask herself. Beyond that it was danger, and she must fly from it.

"I do not want to talk of any of those things to-day," she said, suddenly dropping her parasol between them. "I only want to laugh and be amused, and as you were to devise schemes for my happiness, you must amuse me."

He looked up at her again and he noticed, for all this brave speech, that her hands were trembling as she clutched the handle of her blue parasol.

Triumph and joy ran through him. He could afford to wait a little longer now, since he knew that he must mean something, even perhaps a great deal, to her.

And so for the next half-hour he played with her, he skimmed over the surface of danger, he enthralled her fancy, and with every sentence he threw the glamour of his love around her, and fascinated her soul. All his powers of attraction—and they were many—were employed for her undoing.

And Theodora sat as one in a dream.

At last she felt she *must* wake—must realize that she was not a happy princess, but Theodora, who must live her dull life—and this—and this— where was it leading her to?

So she clasped her hands together suddenly, and she said:

"But do you know we have grown serious, and I asked you to amuse me, Lord Bracondale!"

"I cannot amuse you," he said, lazily, "but shall I tell you about my home, which I should like to show you some day?" And again he began to caress the farthest edge of her dress with his wild flower. Just the smallest movement of smoothing it up and down that no one could resent, but which was disturbing to Theodora. She did not wish him to stop, on the contrary— and yet—

"Yes, I would like to hear of that," she said. "Is it an old, old house?"

"Oh, moderately so, and it has nooks and corners and views that might appeal to you. I believe I should find them all endowed with fresh charm myself, if I could see them with you"—and he made the turning-point of his flower a few inches nearer her hand.

Theodora said nothing; but she took courage and peeped at him again. And she thought how powerful he looked, and how beautifully shaped; and she liked the fineness of the silk of his socks and his shirt, and the cut of his clothes, and the wave of his hair—and last of all, his brown, strong, well-shaped hands.

And then she fell to wondering what the general scheme of things could be that made husbands possess none of these charms; when, if they did, it could all be so good and so delicious, instead of a terribly irksome duty to live with them and be their wives.

"You are not listening to a word I am saying!" said Hector. "Where were your thoughts, cruel lady?"

She was confused a little, and laughed gently. "They were away in a land where you can never come," she said.

He raised himself on his elbow, and supported his head on his hand, while he answered, eagerly:

"But I must come! I want to know them, all your thoughts. Do you know that since we met on Monday you have never been for one instant out of my consciousness. And you would not listen then to what I told you of friendship when it is born of instantaneous sympathy—it is because in some other life two souls have been very near and dear. And that is our case, and I want to make you feel it so, as I do. Tell me that you do—?"

"I do not know what I do feel," said Theodora. "But perhaps—could it be true that we met when we lived before; and when was that? and who were we?"

"It matters not a jot," said he. "So long as you feel it too—that we are not only of yesterday, you and I. There is some stronger link between us."

For one second they looked into each other's eyes, and each read the other's thoughts mirrored there; and if his said, in conscious, passionate words, "I love you," hers were troubled and misty with possibilities. Then she jumped up from her seat suddenly, and her voice trembled a little as she said:

"And now I want to go out of the wood."

He rose too and stood beside her, while he pointed to the glade to the left of the centre they were facing.

"We must penetrate into the future then," he said, "because I told my chauffeur to meet us on the road where I think that will lead to. We cannot go back by the way we have come."

And she did not answer; she was afraid, because she remembered all those avenues were barred by—love.

As he walked beside her, Hector Bracondale knew that now he must be very, very careful in what he said. He must lull her fears to sleep again, or she would be off like a lark towards high heaven, and he would be left upon earth.

So he exerted himself to interest and amuse her in less agitating ways. He talked of his home and his mother and his sister. He wanted Theodora to meet them. She would like Anne, he said, and his mother would love her, he knew. And again the impossible vision same to him, and he felt he hated the face of Morella Winmarleigh.

Usually when he had been greatly attracted by a married woman before, he had unconsciously thought of her as having the qualities which would make her an adorable mistress, a delicious friend, or a holiday amusement. There had never been any reverence mixed up with the affair, which usually had the zest of forbidden fruit, and was hurried along by passion. It had always only depended upon the woman how far he had got beyond these stages; but, as he thought of Theodora, unconsciously a picture always came to him of what she would be were she his wife. And it astonished him when he analyzed it; he, the scoffer at bonds, now to find this picture the fairest in the world!

And as yet he was hardly even dimly growing to realize that fate would turn the anguish of this desire into a chastisement of scorpions for him.

Things had always been so within his grasp.

"We shall go to England on Tuesday," Theodora said, as they sauntered along down the green glade. "It is so strange, you know, but I have never been there."

"Never been to England!" Hector exclaimed, incredulously.

"No!" and she smiled up at him. All was at peace now in her mind, and she dared to look as much as she pleased.

"No. Papa used to go sometimes, but it was too expensive to take the whole family; so we were left at Bruges generally, or at Dieppe, or where we chanced to be. If it was the summer, often we have spent it in a Normandy farm-house."

"Then how have you learned all the things you know?" he asked.

"That was not difficult. I do not know much," she said, gently, "and Sarah taught me in the beginning, and then I went to convents whenever we were in towns, and dear papa was so kind and generous always; no matter how hard up he was he always got the best masters available for me—and for Clementine. Sarah is much older, and even Clementine five years."

"I wonder what on earth you will think of it—England, I mean?" He was deeply interested.

"I am sure I shall love it. We have always spoken of it as home, you know. And papa has often described my grandfather's houses. Both my grandfathers had beautiful houses, it seems, and he says, now that I am rich and cannot ever be a trouble to them, the family might be pleased to see me."

She spoke quite simply. There never was room for bitterness or irony in her tender heart. And Hector looked down upon her, a sort of worship in his eyes.

"Papa's father is dead long ago; it is his brother who owns Beechleigh now," she continued—"Sir Patrick Fitzgerald. They are Irish, of course, but the place is in Cambridgeshire, because it came from his grandmother."

"Yes, I know the old boy," said Hector. "I see him at the turf—a fiery, vile-tempered, thin, old bird, about sixty."

"That sounds like him," said Theodora.

"And so you are going to make all these relations' acquaintance. What an experience it will be, won't it?" His voice was full of sympathy. "But you will stay in London. They are all there now, I suppose?"

"My Grandfather Borringdon, my mother's father, never goes there, I believe; he is very old and delicate, we have heard. But I have written to him—papa wished me to do so; for myself I do not care, because I think he was unkind to my mother, and I shall not like him. It was cruel never to speak to her again—wasn't it?—just because she married papa, whom she loved very much—papa, who is so handsome that he could never have really been a husband, could he?"

Then she blushed deeply, realizing what she had said.

And the quaintness of it caused Hector to smile while he felt its pathos.

How *could* they all have sacrificed this beautiful young life between them! And he slashed off a tall green weed with his stick when he thought of Josiah Brown—his short, stumpy, plebeian figure and bald, shiny head, his common voice, and his pompousness—Josiah Brown, who had now the ordering of her comings and goings, who paid for her clothes and gave her those great pearls—who might touch her and kiss her—might clasp and caress her—

might hold her in his arms, his very own, any moment of the day—or night! Ah, God! that last thought was impossible—unbearable.

And for one second Hector's eyes looked murderous as they glared into the distance—and Theodora glanced up timidly, and asked, in a sympathetic voice: What was it? What ailed him?

"Some day I will tell you," he said. "But not yet."

Then he asked her more about her family and her plans.

They would stay in London at Claridge's for a week or so, and go down to Bessington Hall for Whitsuntide. It would be ready for them then. Josiah had had it all furnished magnificently by one of those people who had taste and ordered well for those who could afford to pay for it. She was rather longing to see it, she said—her future home—and she could have wished she might have chosen the things herself. Not that it mattered much either way.

"I am very ignorant about houses," she explained, "because we never really had one, you see, but I think, perhaps, I would know what was pretty from museums and pictures—and I love all colors and forms."

He felt sure she would know what was pretty. How delightful it would be to watch her playing with his old home! The touches of her gentle fingers would make everything sacred afterwards.

At last they came to the end of the green glade—and temptation again assailed him. He *must* ruffle the peace of her soft eyes once more.

"And here is the barrier," he said, pointing to a board with "*Terrain réservé*" upon it—*Réserveé pour la chasse de Monsieur le Président*, "The barrier which Love keeps—and I want to take him with us as the prince and princess did in the fairy tale."

"Then you must carry him all by yourself," laughed Theodora. "And he will be heavy and tire you, long before we get to Versailles."

This time she was on her guard—and besides they were walking—and he was no longer caressing the edge of her dress with his wild flower; it was almost easy to fence now.

But when they reached the automobile and he bent over to tuck the rug in—and she felt the touch of his hands and perceived the scent of him—the subtle scent, not a perfume hardly, of his coat, or his hair, a wild rush of that passionate disturbance came over her again, making her heart beat and her eyes dilate.

And Hector saw and understood, and bit his lips, and clinched his hands together under the rug, because so great was his own emotion that he feared what he should say or do. He dared not, dared not chance a dismissal from the joy of her presence forever, after this one day.

"I will wait until I know she loves me enough to certainly forgive me—and then, and then—" he said to himself.

But Fate, who was looking on, laughed while she chanted, "The hour is now at hand when these steeds of passion whose reins you have left loose so long will not ask your leave, noble friend, but will carry you whither they will."

XI

They were both a little constrained upon the journey back to Versailles—and both felt it. But when they turned into the Porte St. Antoine Theodora woke up.

"Do you know," she said, "something tells me that for a long, long time I shall not again have such a happy day. It can't be more than half-past five or six—need we go back to the Reservoirs yet? Could we not have tea at the little café by the lake?"

He gave the order to his chauffeur, and then he turned to her.

"I, too, want to prolong it all," he said, "and I want to make you happy—always."

"It is only lately that I have begun to think about things," she said, softly—"about happiness, I mean, and its possibilities and impossibilities. I think before my marriage I must have been half asleep, and very young."

And Hector thought, "You are still, but I shall awake you."

"You see," she continued, "I had never read any novels, or books about life until *Jean d'Agrève*. And now I wonder sometimes if it is possible to be really happy—really, really happy?"

"I know it is," he said; "but only in one way."

She did not dare to ask in what way. She looked down and clasped her hands.

"I once thought," she went on, hurriedly, "that I was perfectly happy the first time Josiah gave me two thousand francs, and told me to go out with my maid and buy just what I wished with it; and oh, we bought everything I could think Sarah and Clementine could want, numbers and numbers of things, and I remember I was fearfully excited when they were sent off to Dieppe. But I never knew if I chose well or if they liked them all quite, and now to do that does not give me nearly so much joy."

Soon they drew up at the little café and ordered tea, which he guessed probably would be very bad and they would not drink. But tea was English, and more novel than coffee for Theodora, and that she must have, she said.

She was so gracious and sweet in the pouring of it out, when presently it came, and the elderly waiter seemed so sympathetic, and it was all gay and bright with the late afternoon sun streaming upon them.

"The garçon takes us for a honeymoon couple," Hector said; "he sees you have beautiful new clothes, and that we have not yet begun to yawn with each other."

But Theodora had not this view of honeymoons. To her a honeymoon meant a nightmare, now happily a thing of the past, and almost forgotten.

"Do not speak of it," she said, and she put out her hands as if to ward off an ugly sight, and Hector bent over the table and touched her fingers gently as he said:

"Forgive me," and he raged within himself. How could he have been so gauche, so clumsy and unlike himself. He had punished them both, and destroyed an illusion. He meant that she should picture herself and him as married lovers, and she had only seen—Josiah Brown. They both fell into silence and so finished their repast.

"I want you to walk now," Hector said, "through some delicious allées where I will show you Encĕlădus after he was struck by the thunders of Zeus. You will like him, I think, and there is fine greensward around him where we can sit awhile."

"I was always sorry for him," said Theodora; "and oh, how I would like to go to Sicily and see Ætna and his fiery breath coming forth, and to know when the island quakes it is the poor giant turning his weary side!"

To go to Sicily—and with her! The picture conjured up in Hector's imagination made him thrill again.

Then he told her about it all, he charmed her fancy and excited her imagination, and by the time they came to their goal the feeling of jar had departed, and the dangerous sense of attraction—of nearness—had returned.

It was nearly seven o'clock, and here among the trees all was in a soft gloom of evening light.

"Is not this still and far away?" he said, as they sat on an old stone bench. "I often stay the whole morning here when I spend a week at Versailles."

"How peaceful and beautiful! Oh, I would like a week here, too!" and Theodora sighed.

"You must not sigh, beautiful princess," he implored, "on this our happy day."

The slender lines of her figure seemed all drooping. She reminded him more than ever of the fragment of Psyche in the Naples Museum.

"No, I must not sigh," she said. "But it seems suddenly to have grown sad—the air—what does it mean? Tell me, you who know so many things?" There was a pathos in her voice like a child in distress.

It communicated itself to him, it touched some chords in his nature hitherto silent. His whole being rushed out to her in tenderness.

"It seems to me it is because the time grows nearer when we must go back to the world. First to dinner with the others, and then—Paris. I would like to stay thus always—just alone with you."

She did not refute this solution of her sadness. She knew it was true. And when he looked into her eyes, the blue was troubled with a mist as of coming tears.

Then passion—more mighty than ever—seized him once more. He only felt a wild desire to comfort her, to kiss away the mist—to talk to her. Ah!

"Theodora!" he said, and his voice vibrated with emotion, while he bent forward and seized both her hands, which he lifted to his face—she had not put on her gloves again after the tea—her cool, little, tender hands! He kissed and kissed their palms.

"Darling—darling," he said, incoherently, "what have I done to make your dear eyes wet? Oh, I love you so, I love you so, and I have only made you sad."

She gave a little, inarticulate cry. If a wounded dove could sob, it might have been the noise of a dove, so beseeching and so pathetic. "Oh, please—you must not," she said. "Oh, what have you done!—you have killed our happy day."

And this was the beginning of his awakening. He sat for many moments with his head buried in his hands. What, indeed, had he done!—and they would be turned out of their garden of Eden—and all because he was a brute, who could not control his passion, but must let it run riot on the first opportunity.

He suffered intensely. Suffered, perhaps, for the first time in his life.

She had not said one word of anger—only that tone in her voice reached to his heart.

He did not move and did not speak, and presently she touched his hands softly with her slender fingers, it seemed like the caress of an angel's wing.

"Listen," she said, so gently. "Oh, you must not grieve—but it was too good to be true, our day. I ought to have known to where we were drifting, I am wicked to have let you say all you have said to-day, but oh, I was asleep,

I think, and I only knew that I was happy. But now you have shown me—and oh, the dream is broken up. Come, let us go back to the world."

Then he raised his eyes to her face, and they were haggard and miserable.

How her simple speech, blaming herself who was all innocent, touched his heart and filled him with shame at his unworthiness.

"Oh, forgive me!" he pleaded. "Oh, please forgive me! I am mad, I think, I love you so—and I had to tell you—and yes, I will say it all now, and then you can punish me. From the first moment I looked into your angel eyes it has been growing, you are so true and so sweet, and so miles beyond all other women in the world. Each minute I have loved you more—and all the time I thought to win you. Yes, you may well turn away, and shrink from me now that you know the brute I am. I thought I would make you love me, and you would forgive me then. But I have suddenly seen your soul, my darling, and I am ashamed, and I can only ask you to forgive me and let me worship you and be your slave—I will not ask for any return—only to worship you and be your slave—that I may show you I am not all brute and may earn your pardon."

And then Theodora's blindness fell from her and she knew that she loved him—she had faced the fact at last. And all over her being there thrilled a mad, wild joy. It surged up and crushed out fear and pain—for just one moment—and then she too, in her turn, covered her face with her hands.

"Oh, hush! hush!" she said. "What have you done—what have we both done!"

It was characteristic of her that now she realized she loved him she did not fence any longer, she never thought of concealing it from him or of blaming him. They were sinners both, he and she equally guilty.

Another woman might have argued, "He is fooling me; perhaps he has said these things before—I must at least hide my own heart," but not Theodora. Her trust was complete—she loved him—therefore he was a perfect knight—and if he was wicked she was wicked too.

Her gentian eyes were full of tears as she let fall her hands and looked at him. "Oh yes, I have been asleep—I should have known from the beginning why, why I wanted to see you so much—I should never have come—and I should have understood in the wood that we could not leave it without bringing Love with us—and now we may not be happy any more."

And then it was his turn to be exalted with wild joy.

"Do you know what you have said," he whispered, breathless. "Your words mean that you love me—Theodora—darling mine." And once again passion blazed in his eyes, and he would have taken her in his arms; but she put up her hands and gently pushed him from her.

"Yes," she said, simply, "I love you, but that only makes it all the harder—and we must say good-bye at once, and go our different ways. You who are so strong and know so much—I trust you, dear—you must help me to do what is right."

She never thought of reproaching him, of telling him, as she very well could have done, that he had taken cruel advantage of her unsophistication. All her mind was full of the fact that they were both very sad and wicked and must help each other.

"I *cannot* say good-bye," he said, "now that I know you love me, darling; it is impossible. How can we part—what will the days be—how could we get through our lives?"

She looked at him, and her eyes were the eyes of a wounded thing—dumb and pitiful, and asking for help.

Then the something that was fine and noble in Hector Bracondale rose up in him—the crust of selfishness and cynicism fell from him like a mask. He suddenly saw himself as he was, and she—as she was—and a determination came over him to grow worthy of her love, obey her slightest wish, even if it must break his heart.

He dropped upon his knees beside her on the greensward, and buried his face in her lap.

"Darling—my queen," he said. "I will do whatever you command—but oh, it need not be good-bye. Don't let me sicken and die out of your presence. I swear, on my word of honor, I will never trouble you. Let me worship you and watch over you and make your life brighter. Oh, God! there can be no sin in that."

"I trust you!" she said, and she touched the waves of his hair. "And now we must not linger—we must come at once out of this place. I—I cannot bear it any more."

And so they went—into an *allée* of close, cropped trees, where the gloom was almost twilight; but if there was pain there was joy too, and almost peace in their hearts.

All the anguish was for the afterwards. Love, who is a god, was too near to his kingdom to admit of any rival.

"Hector," she whispered, and as she said his name a wild thrill ran through him again. "Hector—the Austrian Prince at Armenonville said life was a current down which our barks floated, only to be broken up on the rocks if it was our fate; and I said if we tried very hard some angel would steer us past them into smooth waters beyond; and I want to you to help me to find the angel, dear—will you?"

But all he could say was that she was the angel, the only angel in heaven or earth.

And so they came at last to the Bason de Neptune, and on through the side door into the Réservoirs—and there was the widow's automobile that moment arrived.

XII

Every one behaved with immense propriety—they said just what they should have said, there was no *gêne* at all. And when they went up the stairs together to arrange their hair and their hats for dinner, the elder woman slipped her arm through Theodora's.

"I am going to marry your father, my dear," she said, "and I want you to be the first to wish me joy."

The dinner went off with great gayety. The widow especially was full of bright sayings, and Captain Fitzgerald made the most devoted lover. Not too elated by his good-fortune, and yet thoroughly happy and tender. He continually told himself that fate had been uncommonly kind to mix business and pleasure so dexterously, for if the widow had not possessed a cent, he still would have been glad to marry her.

He had been quite honest with her on their drive, explaining his financial situation and his disadvantages, which he said could only be slightly balanced by his devotion and affection—but of those he would lay the whole at her feet.

And the widow had said:

"Now look here, I am old enough just to know what my money is worth—and if you like to put it as a business speculation for me, I consider, in buying the companion for the rest of my life who happens to suit me, I am laying out the sum to my own advantage."

After that there was no more to be said, and he had spent his time making love to her like any Romeo of twenty, and both were content.

All through dinner a certain strange excitement dominated Theodora. She felt there would be more deep emotion yet to come for her before the day should close.

How were they going back to Paris?

The moon had risen pure and full, she could see it through the windows. The night was soft and warm, and when the last sips of coffee and liqueurs were finished it was still only nine o'clock.

On an occasion when no personal excitement was stirring Captain Fitzgerald he probably would have hesitated about approving of Theodora spending the entire evening alone with Lord Bracondale. She was married, it was true—but to Josiah Brown—and Dominic Fitzgerald knew his world. To-night, however, neither the widow nor he had outside thoughts beyond themselves. Indeed, Mrs. McBride was so overflowing with joy she had almost a feeling of satisfaction in the knowledge that the others would possibly be happy too—when she thought of them at all!

Again she decided the situation for every one, and again fate laughed.

There was no use staying any longer at Versailles, because the park gates were shut and they could not stroll in the moonlight, but a drive back and a few turns in the Bois with a little supper at Madrid would be a fitting ending to the day.

"You must meet us at Madrid at half-past ten," she said; "and Dominic"—the name came out as if from long habit—"telephone for a table in the bosquet—Numero 3—I like that garçon best, he knows my wants."

And so they got into their separate automobiles.

"Let us have all the windows down," said Theodora, "to get all the beautiful air—it is such a lovely night."

Her heart was beating as it had never beat before. How could she control herself! How keep calm and ordinary during the enchanting drive! Her hands were cold as ice, while flaming roses burned in the white velvet cheeks.

And Hector saw it all and understood, and passion surged madly in his veins. For a mile or two there was silence—only the moonlight and the swift rushing through the air, and the wild beating of their hearts. And so they came to the long, dark stretch of wood by St. Cloud. And the devil whispered sophistries and fate continued to laugh. Then passion was too strong for him.

"Darling," he said, and his fine resolutions fled to the winds, while his deep voice was hoarse and broken. "My darling!—God! I love you so—beyond all words or sense—Oh, let us be happy for this one night—we must part afterwards I know, and I will accept that—but just for to-night there can be no sin and no harm in being a little happy—when we are going to pay for it with all the rest of our lives. Let us have the memory of one hour of bliss—the angels themselves could not grudge us that."

One hour of bliss out of a lifetime! Would it be a terrible sin, Theodora wondered, a terrible, unforgivable sin to let him kiss her—to let him hold her just once in his arms.

There was no light in the coupé—he had seen to that—only the great lamps flaring in the road and the moonlight.

She clasped her hands in an agony of emotion. She was but a dove in the net of an experienced fowler, but she did not know or think of that, nor he either. They only knew they loved each other passionately, and this situation was more than they could bear.

"Oh, I trust you!" she said. "If you tell me it is not a terrible sin I will believe you—I do not know—I cannot think—I—"

But she could speak no more because she was in his arms.

The intense, unutterable joy—the maddening, intoxicating bliss of the next hour! To have her there, unresisting—to caress her lips and eyes and hair—to murmur love words—to call her his very own! Nothing in heaven could equal this, and no hell was a price too great to pay—so it seemed to him. It was the supremest moment of his life; and how much more of hers who knew none other, who had never received the kisses of men or thrilled to any touch but his!

After a little she drew herself away and shivered. She knew she was wicked now—very, very wicked—but it was again characteristic of her that having made her decision there was no vacillation about her. The die was cast—for that night they were to be happy, and all the rest of her life should be penitence and atonement.

But to-night there was no room for anything but joy. She had never dreamed in her most secret thoughts of moments so gloriously sweet as these—to have a lover—and such a lover! And it was true—it must be true—that they had lived before, and all this passion was not the growth of one short week.

It seemed as if it was all her life, all her being—it could mean nothing now but Hector—Hector—Hector! And over and over again he made her whisper in his ear that she loved him—nor could she ever tire of hearing him say he worshipped her.

Oh, they were foolish and tender and wonderful, as lovers always are.

He had given his orders beforehand and the chauffeur was a man of intelligence. They drove in the most beautiful *allée* when they came to the Bois—and no incident ruffled the exquisite peace and bliss of their time.

Suddenly Hector became aware of the fact it was just upon half-past ten, and they were almost in sight of Madrid, which would end it all.

And a pang of hideous pain shot through him, and he did not speak.

In the distance the lights blazed into the night, and the sight of them froze Theodora to ice.

It was finished then—their hour of joy.

"My darling," he exclaimed, passionately, "good-bye, and remember all my life is in your hands, and I will spend it in worship of you and thankfulness for this hour of yourself you have given to me. I am yours to do with as you will until death do us part."

"And I," said Theodora, "will never love another man—and if we have sinned we have sinned together—and now, oh, Hector, we must face our fates."

Her voice tore his very heartstrings in its unutterable pathos.

And in that last passionate kiss it seemed as if they exchanged their very souls.

Then they drove into the glare of the restaurant lights, having tasted of the knowledge of good and evil.

XIII

"What have I done? What have I done?" Hector groaned to himself in anguish as he paced up and down his room at the Ritz an hour after the party had broken up, and he had driven Mrs. McBride back in his automobile, leaving hers to father and daughter.

All through supper Theodora had sat limp and white as death, and every time she had looked at him her eyes had reminded him of a fawn he had wounded once at Bracondale, in the park, with his bow and arrow, when he was a little boy. He remembered how fearfully proud he had been as he saw it fall, and then how it had lain in his arms and bled and bled, and its tender eyes had gazed at him in no reproach, only sorrow and pain, and a dumb asking why he had hurt it.

All the light of the stars seemed quenched, no eyes in the world had ever looked so unutterably pathetic as Theodora's eyes, and gradually as they sat and talked platitudes and chaffed with the elderly fiancées, it had come to him how cruel he had been—he who had deliberately used every art to make her love him—and now, having gained his end, what could he do for her? What for himself? Nothing but sorrow faced them both. He had taken brutal advantage of her gentleness and innocence—when chivalry alone should have made him refrain.

He saw himself as he was—the hunter and she the hunted—and the knowledge that he would pay with all the anguish and regret of a passionate, hopeless love—perhaps for the rest of his life—did not balance things to his awakened soul. If his years should be one long, gnawing ache for her, what of hers? And she was so young. His life, at all events, was a free one; but hers tied to Josiah Brown! And this thought drove him to madness. She belonged to Josiah Brown—not to him whom she loved—but to Josiah Brown, plebeian and middle-aged and exacting. He knew now that he ought to have gone away at once, the next day after they had met. His whole course of conduct had been weak and absolutely self-indulgent and wicked.

Who was he to dare to have raised his eyes to this angel, and try to scorch even the hem of her clothing! And now he had only brought suffering upon her and dimmed the light in God's two stars, which were her eyes.

And then wild passion shook him, and he could only live again the divine moments when she had nestled unresisting in his arms. Would it have made things better or worse if he had not yielded to the temptation of that hour of night and solitude?

After all, the sin was in making her love him, not in just holding her and kissing her lips. And at least, at least, they would have that exquisite memory of moments of unutterable bliss to keep for the rest of their lives.

His windows were wide open, and he leaned upon the balcony and gazed out at the moon. What good had all his life been? What benefit had he brought to any one? Then he seemed to see a clear vision of Theodora's short existence. Every picture she had unconsciously shown him was of some gentle thought of unselfishness for others.

And now he had laid a burden upon her shoulders, when he would not hurt a hair of her head—that dear, exquisite head which had lain upon his breast only two hours ago, and could never lie there again. He knew this was the end.

Then anguish and remorse seized him, and he buried his face on his crossed arms.

And Theodora staggered up to her room like one half dead. Mercifully Josiah Brown, had gone to bed, leaving a message with Henriette, Theodora's maid, that on no account was she to make any noise or disturb him.

Henriette adored her mistress—as who did not who served her?—and she felt distressed to see madame so pale. Doubtless madame had had a most tiring day. Madame had, and was thankful when at last she was left alone with her thoughts. Then she, too, opened wide the windows and gazed at the moon.

She had no cause for remorse for evil conduct like Hector. She had made no plans for the entrapping of any soul, and yet she felt forlorn and wicked. Oh yes, she was awake now and knew where she had been drifting. And so love had come at last, and indeed, indeed it meant life. This blast had struck her, and she had been blind in not recognizing it at once.

But oh, how sweet it was!—love—and it seemed as if it could make everything good and fair. If he and she who loved each other could have belonged to each other, surely they might have shed joy and gladness and kindness on all around.

Then she lay on her bed and did not try to reason any more; she only knew she loved Hector Bracondale with all her heart and being, and that she was married to Josiah Brown.

And what would the days be when she never saw him? And he, too, he would be sad—and then there was poor Josiah—who was so generous to her. He could not help being vulgar and unsympathetic, and her duty was to make him happy. Well, she could do that, she would try her very best to do that.

But thrills ran through her with the recollection of the moments in the drive to Paris—oh, why had no one told her or warned her all her life about this good thing love? At last, worn out with all emotions, sleep gently closed her eyes.

And fate up above laughed no more. Her sport was over for a time, she had made a sorry ending to their happy day.

XIV

Josiah had been too much fatigued on his machinery hunt with Mr. Clutterbuck R. Tubbs. They had lunched too richly, he said, and stood about too long, and so all the Sunday he was peevish and fretful, and required Theodora's constant attention. She must sit by his bedside all the morning, and drive round and round all the afternoon.

He told her she was not looking well. These excursions did not suit either of them, and he would be glad to get to England.

He asked a few questions about Versailles, and Theodora vouchsafed no unnecessary information. Nor did she tell him of her father's good-fortune. The widow had expressly asked her not to. She wished it to appear in the New York *Herald* first of all, she said. And they could have a regular rejoicing at the banquet on Monday night.

"Men are all bad," she had told Theodora during their ante-dinner chat. "Selfish brutes most of them; but nature has arranged that we happen to want them, and it is not for me to go against nature. Your father is a gentleman and he keeps me from yawning, and I have enough money to be able to indulge that and whatever other caprices I may have acquired; so I think we shall be happy. But a man in the abstract—don't amount to much!" And Theodora had laughed, but now she wondered if ever she would think it was true. Would Hector ever appear in the light of a caprice she could afford, to keep her from yawning? Could she ever truly say, "He don't amount to much!" Alas! he seemed now to amount to everything in the world.

The unspeakable flatness of the day! The weariness! The sense of all being finished! She did not even allow herself to speculate as to what Hector was doing with himself. She must never let her thoughts turn that way at all if she could help it. She must devote herself to Josiah and to getting through the time. But something had gone out of her life which could never come back, and also something had come in. She was awake—she, too, had lived for one moment like in *Jean d'Agrève*—and it seemed as if the whole world were changed.

Captain Fitzgerald did not appear all day, so the Sunday was composed of unadulterated Josiah. But it was only when Theodora was alone at last late at night, and had opened wide her windows and again looked out on the moon, that a little cry of anguish escaped her, and she remembered she would see Hector to-morrow at the dinner-party. See him casually, as the rest of the guests, and this is how it would be forever—for ever and ever.

Lord Bracondale had passed what he termed a dog's day. He had gone racing, and there had met, and been bitterly reproached by, Esclarmonde de Chartres for his neglect.

Qu'est-ce qu'il a eu pour toute une semaine?

He had important business in England, he said, and was going off at once; but she would find the bracelet she had wished for waiting for her at her apartment, and so they parted friends.

He felt utterly revolted with all that part of his life.

He wanted nothing in the world but Theodora. Theodora to worship and cherish and hold for his own. And each hour that came made all else seem more empty and unmeaning.

Just before dinner he went into the widow's sitting-room. She was alone, Marie had said in the passage—resting, she thought, but madame would certainly see milord. She had given orders for him to be admitted should he come.

"Now sit down near me, beau jeune homme," Mrs. McBride commanded from the depths of her sofa, where she was reclining, arrayed in exquisite billows of chiffon and lace. "I have been expecting you. It is not because I have been indulging in a little sentiment myself that my eyes are glued shut—you have a great deal to confess—and I hope we have not done too much harm between us."

Hector wanted sympathy, and there was something in the widow's directness which he felt would soothe him. He knew her good heart. He could speak freely to her, too, without being troubled by an over-delicacy of *mauvaise honte*, as he would have been with an Englishwoman. It would not have seemed sacrilege to the widow to discuss with him—who was a friend—the finest and most tender sentiments of her own, or any one else's, heart. He drew up a *bergère* and kissed her hand.

"I have been behaving like a damned scoundrel," he said.

"My gracious!" exclaimed Mrs. McBride, with a violent jerk into a sitting position. "You don't say—"

Then, for the first time for many years, a deep scarlet blush overspread Hector's face, even up to his forehead—as he realized how she had read his speech—how most people of the world would have read it. He got up from his chair and walked to the window.

"Oh, good God!" he said, "I don't mean that."

The widow fell back into her pillows with a sigh of relief.

"I mean I have deliberately tried to make her unhappy, and I have succeeded—and myself, too."

"That is not so bad then," and she settled a cushion. "Because unhappiness is only a thing for a time. You are crazy for the moon, and you can't get it, and you grieve and curse for a little, and then a new moon arises. What else?"

"Well, I want you to sympathize with me, and tell me what I had better do. Shall I go back to England to-morrow morning, or stay for the dinner-party?"

"You got as far, then, as telling each other you loved each other madly—and are both suffering from broken hearts, after one week's acquaintance."

"Don't be so brutal!" pleaded Hector.

And she noticed that his face looked haggard and changed. So her shrewd, kind eyes beamed upon him.

"Yes, I dare say it hurts; but having broken up your cake, you can't go on eating it. Why, in Heaven's name, did you let affairs get to a climax?"

"Because I am mad," said Hector, and he stretched out his arms. "I cannot tell you how much I love her. Haven't you seen for yourself what a darling she is? Every dear word she speaks shows her beautiful soul, and it all creeps right into my heart. I worship her as I might an angel, but I want her in my arms."

Mrs. McBride knew the English. They were not emotional or *poseurs* like some other nations, and Hector Bracondale was essentially a man of the world, and rather a whimsical cynic as well. So to see him thus moved must mean great things. She was guilty, too, for helping to create the situation. She must do what she could for him, she felt.

"You should pull yourself together, mon cher Bracondale," she said; "it is not like you to be limp and undecided. You had better stay for the party, and make yourself behave like a gentleman, and how you mean to continue. We have passed the days when 'Oh no, we never mention him' is the order, and 'never meeting,' and that sort of thing. You are bound to meet unless you go into the wilds. And you must face it and try to forget her."

"I can never forget her," he said, in a deep voice; "but, as you say, I must face it and do my best."

"You see," continued the widow, "the girl has only been married a year, and her husband is the most unattractive human being you could find along a sidewalk of miles; but he is her husband, anyway, and she may have children."

Hector clinched his hands in a convulsive movement of anguish and rage.

"And you must realize all these possibilities, and settle a path for yourself and stick to it."

"Oh, I couldn't bear that!" he said. "It would be better I should take her away myself now, to-day."

"You will do no such thing!" said the widow, sternly, and she sat up again. "You forget I am going to marry her father, and I shall look upon her as my daughter and protect her from wolves—do you hear? And what is more, she is too good and true to go with you. She has a backbone if you haven't; and she'll see it her duty to stick to that lump of middle-class meat she is bound to—and she'll do her best, if she suffers to heart-break. It is she, the poor, little white dove, that you and I have wounded between us, that I pity, not you—great, strong man!"

Mrs. McBride's eyes flashed.

"Oh, you are all the same, you Englishmen. Beasts to kill and women to subjugate—the only aims in life!"

"Don't!" said Hector. "I am not the animal you think me. I worship Theodora, and I would devote my life and its best aims to secure her happiness and do her honor; but don't you see you have drawn a picture that would drive any man mad—"

"I said you had to face the worst, and I calculate the worst for you would be to see her with some little Browns along. My! How it makes you wince! Well, face it then and be a man."

He sat for a moment, his head buried in his hands—then—

"I will," he said, "I will do what I can; but oh, when you have the chance you will be good to her, won't you, dear friend?"

"There, there!" said the widow, and she patted his hand. "I had to scold you, because I see you have got the attack very badly and only strong measures are any good; but you know I am sorry for you both, and feel dreadfully, because I helped you to it without enough thought as to consequences."

There was silence for a few minutes, and she continued to stroke his hand.

"Dominic has run down to Dieppe to see those daughters of his," she said, presently, "and won't be back to-night. I meant to be all alone and meditate and go to bed early; but you can dine with me, if you wish, up here, and we will talk everything over. Our plans for the future, I mean, and what will be best to do; I kind of feel like your mother-in-law, you know." Which sentence comforted him.

This woman was his friend, and so kind of heart, if sometimes a little plain-spoken.

And late that night he wrote to Theodora.

"My darling," he began. "I must call you that even though I have no right to. *My* darling—I want to tell you these my thoughts to-night, before I see you to-morrow as an ordinary guest at your dinner-party. I want you to know how utterly I love you, and how I am going to do my best with the rest of my life to show you how I honor you and revered you as an angel, and something to live for and shape my aims to be worthy of the recollection of that hour of bliss you granted me. Dearest love, does it not give you joy—just a little—to remember those moments of heaven? I do not regret anything, though I am all to blame, for I knew from the beginning I loved you, and just where love would lead us. But it was not until I saw the peep into your soul, when you never reproached me, that I began to understand what a brute I had been—how unworthy of you or your love. Darling, I don't ask you to try and forget me—indeed, I implore you not to do so. I think and believe you are of the nature which only loves once in a lifetime, and I am world-worn and experienced enough to know I have never really loved before. How passionately I do now I cannot put into words. So let us keep our love sacred in our hearts, my darling, and the knowledge of it will comfort and soothe the anguish of separation. Beloved one, I am always thinking of you, and I want to tell you my vision of heaven would be to possess you for my wife. My happiest dream will always be that you are there—at Bracondale—queen of my home and my heart, darling. *My* darling! But however it may be, whether you decide to chase away every thought of me or not, I want you to know I will go on worshipping you, and doing my utmost to serve you with my life.—For ever and ever your devoted lover."

And then he signed it "Hector," and not "Bracondale."

The widow had promised to give it into Theodora's own hand on the morrow.

He added a postscript:

"I want you to meet my mother and my sister in London. Will you let me arrange it? I think you will like Anne. And oh, more than all I want you to come to Bracondale. Write me your answer that I may have your words to keep always."

Mrs. McBride came round in the morning to the private hotel in the Avenue du Bois, to ask the exact time of the dinner-party, she said. She wanted to see for herself how things were going. And the look in Theodora's eyes grieved her.

"I am afraid it has gone rather deeply with her," she mused. "Now what can I do?"

Theodora was unusually sweet and gentle, and talked brightly of how glad she was for her father's happiness, and of their plans about England; but all the time Jane McBride was conscious that the something which had made her eyes those stars of gracious happiness was changed—instead there was a deep pathos in them, and it made her uncomfortable.

"I wish to goodness I had let well alone, and not tried to give her a happy day," she said to herself.

Just before leaving, she slipped Hector's letter into Theodora's hand. "Lord Bracondale asked me to give you this, my child," she said, and she kissed her. "And if you will write the answer, will you post it to him to the Ritz."

All over Theodora there rushed an emotion when she took the letter. Her hands trembled, and she slipped it into the bodice of her dress. She would not be able to read it yet. She was waiting, all ready dressed, for Josiah to enter any moment, to take their usual walk in the Bois.

Then she wondered what would the widow think of her action, slipping it into her dress—but it was done now, and too late to alter. And their eyes met, and she understood that her future step-mother was wide awake and knew a good many things. But the kind woman put her arm round her and kissed her soft cheek.

"I want you to be my little daughter, Theodora," she said. "And if you have a heartache, dear, why I have had them, too—and I'd like to comfort you. There!"

XV

The dinner-party went off with great éclat. Had not all the guests read in the New York *Herald* that morning of Captain Fitzgerald's good-fortune? He with his usual *savoir-vivre* had arranged matters to perfection. The company was chosen from among the nicest of his and Mrs. McBride's friends.

The invitations had been couched in this form: "I want you to meet my daughter, Mrs. Josiah Brown, my dear lady," or "dear fellow," as the case might be. "She is having a little dinner at Madrid on Monday night, and so hopes you will let me persuade you to come."

And the French Count, and Mr. Clutterbuck R. Tubbs and his daughter, Theodora had asked herself. Also the Austrian Prince. The party consisted of about twenty people—and the menu and the Tziganes were as perfect as they could be, while the night might have been a night of July—it happened to be that year when Paris was blessed with a gloriously warm May.

Lord Braconwdale was late: had not the post come in just as he was starting, and brought him a letter, whose writing, although he had never seen it before, filled him with thrills of joy.

Theodora had found time during the day to read and reread his epistle, and to kiss it more than once with a guilty blush.

And she had written this answer:

> "I have received your letter, and it says many things to me—and, Hector, it will comfort me always, this dear letter, and to know you love me.
>
> "I have led a very ordinary life, you see, and the great blast of love has never come my way, or to any one whom I knew. I did not realize, quite, it was a real thing out of books—but now I know it is; and oh, I can believe, if circumstances were different, it could be heaven. But this cannot alter the fact that for me to think of you much would be very wrong now. I do love you—I do not deny it—though I am going to try my utmost to put the thought away from me and to live my life as best I can. I do not regret anything either, dear, because, but for you, I would never have known what life's meaning is at all—I should have stayed asleep always; and you have opened my eyes and taught me to see new beauties in all nature. And oh, we must not grieve, we must thank fate for giving us this one peep

into paradise—and we must try and find the angel to steer our barks for us beyond the rocks. Listen—I want you to do something for me to-night. I want you not to look at me much, or tempt me with your dear voice. It will be terribly hard in any case, but if you will be kind you will help me to get through with it, and then, and then—I hardly dare to look ahead—but I leave it all in your hands. I would like to meet your mother and sister—but when, and where? I feel inclined to say, not yet, only I know that is just cowardice, and a shrinking from possible pain in seeing you. So I leave it to you to do what is best, and I trust to your honor and your love not to tempt me beyond bearing-point—and remember, I am trying, trying hard, to do what is right—and trying not to love you.

"And so, good-bye. I must never say this again—or even think it unsaid; but to-night, oh! Yes, Hector, know that I love you! THEODORA."

And all the way to Madrid, as he flew along in his automobile, his heart rejoiced at this one sentence—"Yes, Hector, know that I love you!"

The rest of the world did not seem to matter very much. How fortunate it is that so often Providence lets us live on the pleasure of the moment!

He sat on her left hand—the Austrian Prince was on her right—and studiously all through the repast he tried to follow her wishes and the law he had laid down for himself as the pattern of his future conduct.

He was gravely polite, he never turned the conversation away from the general company, including her neighbors in it all the time, and only when he was certain she was not noticing did he feast his eyes upon her face.

She was looking supremely beautiful. If possible, whiter than usual, and there was a shadow in her eyes as of mystery, which had not been there before—and while their pathos wrung his heart, he could not help perceiving their added beauty. And he had planted this change there—he, and he alone. He admired her perfect taste in dress—she was all in pure white, muslin and laces, and he knew it was of the best, and the creation of the greatest artist.

She looked just what *his* wife ought to look, infinitely refined and slender and stately and fair.

Morella Winmarleigh would seem as a large dun cow beside her.

Then suddenly they both remembered it was only a week this night since they had met. Only seven days in which fate had altered all their lives.

The Austrian Prince wondered to himself what had happened. He had not been blind to the situation at Armenonville, and here they seemed like polite hostess and guest, nothing more.

"They are English, and they are very well bred, and they are very good actors," he thought. "But, mon Dieu! were I ce beau jeune homme!"

And so it had come to an end—the feast and the Tziganes playing, and Theodora will always be haunted by that last wild Hungarian tune. Music, which moved every fibre of her being at all times, to-night was a torture of pain and longing. And he was so near, so near and yet so far, and it seemed as if the music meant love and separation and passionate regret, and the last air most passionate of all, and before the final notes died away Hector bent over to her, and he whispered:

"I have got your letter, and I love you, and I will obey its every wish. You must trust me unto death. Darling, good-night, but never good-bye!"

And she had not answered, but her breath had come quickly, and she had looked once in his eyes and then away into the night.

And so they shook hands politely and parted. And next day Mr. and Mrs. Josiah Brown crossed over to England.

XVI

It was pouring with rain the evening Lord Bracondale arrived from Paris at the family mansion in St. James's Square. He had only wired at the last moment to his mother, too late to change her plans; she was unfortunately engaged to take Morella Winmarleigh to the opera, and was dining early at that lady's house, so she could only see him for a few moments in her dressing-room before she started.

"My darling, darling boy!" she exclaimed, as he opened the door and peeped in. "Streatfield, bring that chair for his lordship, and—oh, you can go for a few minutes."

Then she folded him in her arms, and almost sobbed with joy to see him again.

"Well, mother," he said, when she had kissed him and murmured over him as much as she wished. "Here I am, and what a sickening climate! And where are you off to?"

"I am going to dine with Morella Winmarleigh," said Lady Bracondale, "early, to go to the opera, and then I shall take her on to the Brantingham's ball. Won't you join us at either place, Hector? I feel it so dreadfully, having to rush off like this, your first evening, darling."

She stood back and looked at him. She must see for herself whether he was well, and if this riotous life she feared he had been leading lately had not too greatly told upon him. Her fond eyes detected an air of weariness: he looked haggard, and not so full of spirits as he usually was. Alas! if he would only stay in England!

"I am rather tired, mother; I may look in at the opera, but I can't face a ball. How is Anne, and what is she doing to-night?" he said.

"Anne has a bad cold. We have had such weather—nothing but rain since Sunday night! She is dining at home and going to bed early. I have just had a telephone message from her; she is longing to see you, too."

"I think I shall go round and dine with her then," said Hector, "and join you later."

They talked on for about ten minutes before he left her to dress, running against Streatfield in the passage. She had known him since his birth, and beamed with joy at his return.

He chaffed her about growing fat, and went on his way to telephone to his sister.

"His lordship looks pale, my lady," said the demure woman, as she fastened Lady Bracondale's bracelet. She, too, disapproved of Paris and bachelorhood, but she did not love Morella Winmarleigh.

"Oh, you think so, Streatfield?" Lady Bracondale exclaimed, in a worried voice. "Now that we have got him back we must take great care of him. His lordship will join me at the opera. Are you sure he likes those aigrettes in my hair?"

"Why, it's one of his lordship's favorite styles, my lady. You need have no fears," said the maid.

And thus comforted, Lady Bracondale descended the great staircase to her carriage.

She was still a beautiful woman, though well past fifty. Her splendid, dark hair had hardly a thread of gray in it, and grew luxuriantly, but she insisted upon wearing it simply parted in the middle and coiled in a mass of plaits behind, while one braid stood up coronet fashion well at the back of her head. She was addicted to rich satins and velvets, and had a general air of Victorian repose and decorum. There was no attempt to retain departed youth; no golden wigs or red and white paint disfigured her person, which had an immense natural dignity and stateliness. It made her shiver to see some of her contemporaries dressed and arranged to represent not more than twenty years of age. But so many modern ways of thought and life jarred upon her!

"Mother is still in the early seventies; she has never advanced a step since she came out," Anne always said, "and I dare say she was behind the times even then."

Meanwhile, Hector was dressing in his luxurious mahogany-panelled room. Everything in the house was solid and prosperous, as befitted a family who had had few reverses and sufficient perspicacity to marry a rich heiress now and then at right moments in their history.

This early Georgian house had been in the then Lady Bracondale's dower, and still retained its fine carvings and Old-World state.

"How shall I see her again?" was all the thought which ran in Lord Bracondale's head.

"She won't be at a ball, but she might chance to have thought of the opera. It would be a place Mr. Brown would like to exhibit her at. I shall certainly go."

Lady Anningford was tucked up on a sofa in her little sitting-room when her brother arrived at her charming house in Charles Street. Her husband had been sent off to a dinner without her, and she was expecting her brother with impatience. She loved Hector as many sisters do a handsome, popular brother, but rather more than that, and she had fine senses and understood him.

She did not cover him with caresses and endearments when she saw him; she never did.

"Poor Hector has enough of them from mother," she explained, when Monica Ellerwood asked her once why she was so cold. "And men don't care for those sort of things, except from some one else's sister or wife."

"Dear old boy!" was all she said as he came in. "I am glad to see you back."

Then in a moment or two they went down to dinner, talking of various things. And all through it, while the servants were in the room, she prattled about Paris and their friends and the gossip of the day; and she had a shocking cold in her head, too, and might well have been forgiven for being dull.

But when they were at last alone, back in the little sitting-room, she looked at him hard, and her voice, which was rather deep like his, grew full of tenderness as she asked: "What is it, Hector? Tell me about it if I can help you."

He got up and stood with his back to the wood fire, which sparkled in the grate, comforting the eye with its brightness, while the wind and rain moaned outside.

"You can't help me, Anne; no one can," he said. "I have been rather badly burned, but there is nothing to be done. It is my own fault—so one must just bear it."

"Is it the—eh—the Frenchwoman?" his sister asked, gently.

"Good Lord, no!"

"Or the American Monica came back so full of?"

"The American? What American? Surely she did not mean my dear Mrs. McBride?"

"I don't know her name," Anne said, "and I don't want you to say a thing about it, dear, if I can't help you; only it just grieves me to see you looking so sad and distrait, so I felt I must try if there is anything I can do for you. Mother has been on thorns and dying of fuss over this Frenchwoman and the diamond chain—("How the devil did she hear about that?" thought Hector)—until Monica came back with a tale of your devotion to an American."

"One would think I was eighteen years old and in leading-strings still, upon my word," he interrupted, with an irritated laugh. "When will she realize I can take care of myself?"

"Never," said Lady Anningford, "until you have married Morella Winmarleigh; then she would feel you were in good hands."

He laughed again—bitterly this time.

"Morella Winmarleigh! I would not be faithful to her for a week!"

"I wonder if you would be faithful to any woman, Hector? I have often thought you do not know what it means to love—really to love."

"You were perfectly right once. I did not know," he said; "and perhaps I don't now, unless to feel the whole world is a sickening blank without one woman is to love—really to love."

Anne noticed the weariness of his pose and the vibration in his deep voice. She was stirred and interested as she had never been. This dear brother of hers was not wont to care very much. In the past it had always been the women who had sighed and longed and he who had been amused and pleased. She could not remember a single occasion in the last ten years when he had seemed to suffer, although she had seen him apparently devoted to numbers of women.

"And what are you going to do?" she asked, with sympathy, "She is married, of course?"

"Yes."

"Hector, don't you want me to speak about it?"

He took a chair now by his sister's sofa, and he began to turn over the papers rather fast which lay on a table near by.

"Yes, I do," he said, "because, after all, you can do something for me. I want you to be particularly kind to her, will you, Anne, dear?"

"But, of course; only you must tell me who she is and where I shall find her."

"You will find her at Claridge's, and she is only the wife of an impossible Australian millionaire called Brown—Josiah Brown."

"Poor dear Hector, how terrible!" thought Anne. "It is not the American, then?" she said, aloud.

"There never was any American," he exclaimed. "Monica is the most ridiculous gossip, and always sees wrong. If she had not Jack to keep her from talking so much she would not leave one of us with a rag of character."

"I will go to-morrow and call there, Hector," Lady Anningford said. "My cold is sure to be better; and if she is not in, shall I write a note and ask her to lunch? The husband, too, I suppose?"

"I fear so. Anne, you are a brick."

Then he said good-night, and went to the opera.

Left to herself, Lady Anningford thought: "I suppose she is some flashy, pretty creature who has caught Hector's fancy, the poor darling. One never has chanced to find an Australian quite, quite a lady. I almost wish he would marry Morella and have done with it."

Then she lay on her sofa and pondered many things.

She was a year older than her brother, and they had always been the closest friends and comrades.

Lady Anningford was more or less a happy and contented woman now, but there had been moments in her life scorched by passion and infinite pain. Long ago in the beginning when she first came out she had had the misfortune to fall in love with Cyril Lamont, married and bad and attractive. It had given him great pleasure to evade the eye of Lady Bracondale, pure dragon and strict disciplinarian. Anne was a good girl, but she was eighteen years old and had tasted no joy. She was not an easy prey, and her first year had passed in storms of emotion suppressed to the best of her powers.

The situation had been full of shades and contrasts. The outward, a strictly guarded lamb, the life of the world and aristocratic propriety; and the inward, a daily growing mad love for an impossible person, snatched and secret meetings after tea in country-houses, walks in Kensington Gardens, rides along lonely lanes out hunting, and, finally, the brink of complete ruin and catastrophe—but for Hector.

"Where should I be now but for Hector?" her thoughts ran.

Hector was just leaving Eton in those days, and had come up and discovered matters, while she sobbed in his arms, at the beginning of her second season. He had comforted her and never scolded a word, and then he had gone out armed with a heavy hunting-crop, found Cyril Lamont, and had thrashed the man within an inch of his life. It was one of Hector's pleasantest recollections, the thought of his cowering form, his green silk smoking-jacket all torn, and his eyes sightless. Cyril Lamont's talents had not run in the art of self-defence, and he had been very soon powerless in the hands of this young athlete.

The Lamonts went abroad that night, and stayed there for quite six months, during which time Anne mended her broken heart and saw the folly of her ways.

Hector and she had never alluded to the matter all these years, only they were intimate friends and understood each other.

Lady Bracondale adored Hector and was fond of Anne, but had no comprehension of either. Anne was a *frondeuse*, while her mother's mind was fashioned in carved lines and strict boundaries of thought and action.

XVII

Meanwhile, Hector reached the opera, and made his way to the omnibus box where he had his seat.

He felt he could not stand Morella Winmarleigh just yet. The second act of "Faust" was almost over, and with his glass he swept the rows of boxes in vain to find Theodora. He sat a few minutes, but restlessness seized him. He must go to the other side and ascertain if she could be discovered from there. Morella Winmarleigh's box commanded a good view for this purpose, so after all he would face her.

He looked up at her opposite. She sat there with his mother, and she seemed more thoroughly wholesomely unattractive than ever to him.

He hated that shade of turquoise blue she was so fond of, and those unmeaning bits and bows she had stuck about. She was a large young woman with a stolid English fairness.

Her hair had the flaxen ends and sandy roots one so often sees in those women whose locks have been golden as children. It was a thin, dank kind of hair, too, with no glints anywhere. Her eyes were blue and large and meaningless and rather prominent, and her lightish eyelashes seemed to give no shade to them.

Morella's orbs just looked out at you like the bow-windows of a sea-side villa—staring and commonplace. Her features were regular, and her complexion, if somewhat all too red, was fresh withal; so that, possessing an income of many thousands, she passed for a beauty of exceptional merit.

She had a good maid who used her fingers dexterously, and did what she could with a mistress devoid of all sense of form or color.

Miss Winmarleigh went to the opera regularly and sat solidly through it. The music said nothing to her, but it was the right place for her to be, and she could talk to her friends before going on to the numerous balls she attended.

If she loved anything in the world she loved Hector Bracondale, but her feelings gave her no anxieties. He would certainly marry her presently, the affair would be so suitable to all parties; meanwhile, there was plenty of time, and all was in order. The perfect method of her account-books, in which the last sixpence she spent in the day was duly entered, translated itself to her life. Method and order were its watchwords; and if the people who knew her intimately—such as her chaperon, Mrs. Herrick, and her maid, Gibson—thought her mean, she was not aware of their opinion, and went her way in solid rejoicing.

Lady Bracondale was really attached to her. Morella's decorum, her absence of all daring thought in conversation, pleased her so. She had none of that feeling when with Miss Winmarleigh she suffered in the company of her daughter Anne, who said things so often she did not quite understand, yet which she dimly felt might have two meanings, and one of them a meaning she most probably would disapprove of.

She loved Anne, of course, but oh, that she could have been more like herself or Morella Winmarleigh!

Both women saw Hector in the omnibus box, and saw him leave it, and were quite ready with their greetings when he joined them.

Miss Winmarleigh had a slight air of proprietorship about her, which every one knew when Hector was there. And most people thought as she did, that he would certainly marry her in the near future.

He was glad it was not between the acts—there was no excuse for conversation after their greeting, so he searched the house in peace with his glasses.

And although he was hoping to see Theodora, his heart gave a great bound of surprised joy when, on the pit tier, almost next the box he had just left, he discovered her. He supposed it was a box often let to strangers that season, as he could not remember whose the name was as he had passed. He got back into the shadow, that his gaze should not be too remarkable. She had not caught sight of him yet, or so it seemed.

There she sat with her husband and another woman, whom he recognized as one of those kind creatures who go everywhere in society and help strangers when suitably compensated for their trouble.

Where on earth could she have come across Mrs. Devlyn? he wondered. A poisonous woman, who would fill her ears with tales of all the world. Then he guessed, and rightly, the introduction had been effected by Captain Fitzgerald, who would probably have known her in his own day.

Theodora appeared wrapped in the music, and was an enthralling picture of loveliness; her fineness seemed to make all the women's faces who were near look coarse, and her whiteness turned them into gypsies. She wore a gown of black velvet with no relief whatever, only her dazzling skin and her great pearls. He feasted his eyes upon her—eyes hungry with a week's abstinence; for he had felt it more prudent to remain in Paris for some days after she had left.

He looked round the rest of the house, and understood all the other men could, and probably would, gaze too. And then he began to feel hot and jealous! This was different from Paris, where she was more or less a tourist;

but here, how long would she be left in peace without siege being laid to her? He knew his world and the men it contained. Yes, at that moment the door at the back of the box opened and Delaval Stirling came in, Josiah Brown making way for him to sit in front. Delaval Stirling—this was too much!

And Theodora turned with her adorable smile and greeted him, so it showed they had met before—greeted him with pleasure. Good God! How much could happen in a week! Why had he stayed in Paris?

If Morella Winmarleigh had glanced round at his face, even her thick perceptions must have grasped the disturbance which was marked there, as he stood back in the shadow and gazed with angry eyes.

The moment she had seen him come into the box Mrs. Devlyn had said, "I want you to notice a man over there, Mrs. Brown, in the box exactly opposite; on the grand tier—do you see?"

"Yes," said Theodora, and she perceived him shaking hands with Miss Winmarleigh before he caught sight of her, so she was forearmed and turned to the stage.

"He is nice-looking, don't you think so?" continued Mrs. Devlyn, without a pause. "He is going to marry that girl in the box; she is one of the richest heiresses of the day—Miss Winmarleigh. I always point out Hector Bracondale to strangers or foreigners; he is quite a show Englishman."

"Bracondale? Lord Bracondale?" interrupted Josiah Brown. "We met him in Paris, did we not, my love?" turning to Theodora. "He dined with us our last evening. Where is he?"

"Oh, you know him, then!" said Mrs. Devlyn, disappointed. "I wanted to be the first to point him out to you. They will make a handsome pair, won't they—he and Miss Winmarleigh?"

"Very," said Theodora, listlessly, with an air of dragging her thoughts from the music with difficulty, while she suddenly felt sick and cold.

"And are they to be married soon?"

"I don't know exactly; but it has been going on for years, and we all look upon it as a settled thing. She is always about with his mother."

"Is that Lord Bracondale's mother—the lady with the coronet of plaits and the huge white aigrette with the diamond drops in it?" Theodora asked. Her voice was schooled, and had no special tones in it. But oh, how she was thrilling with interest and excitement underneath!

"Yes, that is Lady Bracondale. She is quite a type; always dresses in that old-fashioned way, and won't know a soul who is not of her own set. She is a cousin of one of my husband's aunts. I must introduce you to her."

"She looks pretty haughty," announced Josiah Brown. "I should not care to tread on her toes much." And then he remembered he had seen her years ago driving through the little town of Bracondale.

Theodora asked no more questions. She kept her eyes fixed on the stage, but she knew Hector had raised his glasses now and was scanning the box, and had probably seen her.

What ought it to matter to her that he should be going to marry Miss Winmarleigh? He could be nothing to her—only—only—but perhaps it was not true. This woman, Mrs. Devlyn, whom she began to feel she should dislike very much, had said it was looked upon as settled, not that it was a fact. How could a man be going to marry one woman and make desperate love to another at the same time? It was impossible—and yet—she would *not* look in any case. She would not once raise her eyes that way.

And so in these two boxes green jealousy held sway, and while Hector glared across at Theodora she smiled at Delaval Stirling, and spoke softly of the music and the voices, though her heart was torn with pain.

"Do you see Hector Bracondale is back again, Delaval?" Mrs. Devlyn said. "Do you know why he stayed in Paris so long? I heard—" And she whispered low, so that Theodora only caught the name "Esclarmonde de Chartres" and their modulated mocking laughter.

How they jarred upon her! How she felt she should hate London among all these people whose ways she did not know! She turned a little, and Josiah's vulgar familiar face seemed a relief to her, and her tender eyes melted in kindliness as she looked at him.

"You are very pale to-night, my love," he said. "Would you like to go home?"

But this she would not agree to, and pulled herself together and tried to talk gayly when the curtain went down.

And Hector blamed his own folly for having come up to this box at all. Here he must be glued certainly for a few moments; now that they could talk, politeness could not permit him to fly off at once.

"The house is very full," Miss Winmarleigh said—it was a remark she always made on big nights—"and yet hardly any new faces about."

"Yes," said Hector.

"Does it compare with the Opera-House in Paris, Hector?" Miss Winmarleigh hardly ever went abroad.

"No," said Hector.—Not only had Delaval Stirling retained his seat, but Chris Harford, Mrs. Devlyn's brother, had entered the box now and was assiduously paying his court. "Damned impertinence of the woman, forcing her relations upon them like that," he thought.—"Oh—er—no—that is, I think the Paris Opera-House is a beastly place," he said, absently, "a dull, heavy drab brown and dirty gilding, and all the women look hideous in it."

"Really," said Morella. "I thought everything in Paris was lovely."

"You should go over and see for yourself," he said, "then you could judge. I think most things there are lovely, though."

Miss Winmarleigh raised her glasses now and examined the house. Her eyes lighted at last on Theodora.

"Dear Lady Bracondale," she said, "do look at that woman in black velvet. What splendid pearls! Do you think they are real? Who is it, I wonder, with Florence Devlyn?"

But Hector felt he could not stay and hear their remarks about his darling, so he got up, and, murmuring he must have a talk to his friends in the house, left the box.

He was thankful at least Theodora was sitting on the pit tier—he could walk along the gangway and talk to her from the front.

She saw him coming and was prepared, so no wild roses tinged her cheeks, and her greeting was gravely courteous, that was all.

An icy feeling crept over him. What was the change, this subtle change in voice and eyes? He suddenly had the agonizing sensation of being a great way off from her, shut out of paradise—a stranger. What had happened? What had he done?

Every one knows the Opera-House, and where he would be standing, and the impossibility of saying anything but the most banal commonplaces, looking up like that.

Then Josiah leaned forward, proud of his acquaintanceship with a peer, and said in a distinct voice:

"Won't you come into the box, Lord Bracondale? There is plenty of room." He had not taken to either Delaval Stirling or Chris Harford, and thought a change of company would not come amiss. They had ignored him, and should pay for it.

Hector made his way joyfully to the back, and, entering, was greeted affably by his host, so the other two men got up to leave to make room for him.

He sat down behind Theodora, and Mrs. Devlyn saw it would be wiser to conciliate Josiah by her interested conversation.

She hoped to make a good thing out of this millionaire and his unknown wife, and it would not do to ruffle him at this stage of the affair.

Theodora hardly turned, thus Hector was obliged to lean quite forward to speak to her.

"I have seen my sister to-night," he said, "and she wants so much to meet you. I said perhaps she would find you to-morrow. Will you be at home in the afternoon any time?"

"I expect so," replied Theodora. She was longing to face him, to ask him if it was true he was going to marry that large, pink-faced young woman opposite, who was now staring down upon them with fixed opera-glasses; but she felt frozen, and her voice was a frozen voice.

Hector became more and more unhappy. He tried several subjects. He told her the last news of her father and Mrs. McBride. She answered them all with the same politeness, until, maddened beyond bearing, he leaned still farther forward and whispered in her ear:

"For God's sake, what is it? What have I done?"

"Nothing," said Theodora. What right had she to ask him any question, when for these seven nights and days since they had parted she had been disciplining herself not to think of him in any way? She must never let him know it could matter to her now.

"Nothing? Then why are you so changed? Ah, how it hurts!" he whispered, passionately. And she turned and looked at him, and he saw that her beautiful eyes were no longer those pure depths of blue sky in which he could read love and faith, but were full of mist, as of a curtain between them.

He put his hand up to touch the little gold case he carried always now in his waistcoat-pocket, which contained her letter. He wanted to assure himself it was there, and she had written it—and it was not all a dream.

Theodora's tender heart was wrung by the passionate distress in his eyes.

"Is that your mother over there you were with?" she asked, more gently. "How beautiful she is!"

"Yes," he said, "my mother and Morella Winmarleigh, whom the world in general and my mother in particular have decided I am going to marry."

She did not speak. She felt suddenly ashamed she could ever have doubted him; it must be the warping atmosphere of Mrs. Devlyn's society for these last days which had planted thoughts, so foreign to her nature, in her. She did not yet know it was jealousy pure and simple, which attacks the sweetest, as well, as the bitterest, soul among us all. But a thrill of gladness ran through her as well as shame.

"And aren't you going to marry her, then?" she said, at last. "She is very handsome."

Hector looked at her, and a wave of joy chased out the pain he had suffered. That was it, then! They had told her this already, and she hated it—she cared for him still.

"Surely you need not ask me," he said, deep reproach in his eyes. "You must be very changed in seven days to even have thought it possible."

The shame deepened in Theodora. She was, indeed, unlike herself to have been moved at all by Mrs. Devlyn's words, but she would never doubt again, and she must tell him that.

"Forgive me," she said, quite low, while she looked away. "I—of course I ought to be pleased at anything which made you happy, but—oh, I hated it!"

"Theodora," he said, "I ask you—do not act with me ever—to what end? We know each other's hearts, and I hope it would pain you were I to marry any other woman, as much as in like circumstances it would pain me."

"Yes, it would pain me," she said, simply. "But, oh, we must not speak thus! Please, please talk of the music, or the—the—oh, anything but ourselves."

And he tried hard for the few moments which remained before the curtain rose again. Tried hard, but it was all dust and ashes; and as he left the box and returned to his own seat next door his heart felt like lead. How would he be able to follow the rules he had laid down for himself during his week of meditations in Paris alone?

"You see, dear Lady Bracondale," Morella Winmarleigh had been saying, "Hector knows that woman with the pearls. He is sitting talking to her now."

"Hector knows every one, Morella. Lend me your glasses, mine do not seem to work to-night. Yes, I suppose by some she would be considered pretty," Lady Bracondale continued, when the lorgnette was fixed to her focus. "What do you think, dear?"

"Pretty!" exclaimed Miss Winmarleigh. "Oh no! Much too white, and, oh—er—foreign-looking. We must find out who she is."

The matter was not difficult. Half the house had been interested in the new-comer, the beautiful new-comer with the wonderful pearls, who must be worth while in some way, or she would not be under the wing of Florence Devlyn.

By the time Hector again entered their box in the last act, Miss Winmarleigh had obtained all the information she wanted from one of the many visitors who came to pay their court to the heiress. And the information reassured her. Only the wife of a colonial millionaire; no one of her world or who could trouble her.

Early next morning, while she sat in her white flannel dressing-gown, her hair screwed in curling-pins, after the Brantinghams' ball, she wrote in her journal the customary summary of her day, and ended with: "H.B. returned—same as usual, running after a new woman, nobody of importance; but I had better watch it, and clinch matters between him and me before Goodwood. Ordered the pink silk after all, from the new little dressmaker, and beat her down three pounds as to price. Begun Marvaloso hair tonic."

Then, as it was broad daylight, after carefully replacing in its drawer this locked chronicle of her maiden thoughts, she retired to bed, to sleep the sleep of those just persons whose digestions are as strong as their absence of imagination.

XVIII

Next day Lady Anningford called, as she had promised, at Claridge's, and found Mrs. Brown at home, although it was only three o'clock in the afternoon.

She had not two minutes to wait in the well-furnished first-floor sitting-room, but during that time she noticed there were one or two things about which showed the present occupant was a woman of taste, and there were such quantities of flowers. Flowers, flowers, everywhere.

Theodora entered already dressed for her afternoon drive. She came forward with that perfect grace which characterized her every movement.

If she felt very timid and nervous it did not show in her sweet face, and Lady Anningford perceived Hector had every excuse for his infatuation.

"I am so fortunate to find you at home, Mrs. Brown," she said. "My brother has told me so much about you, and I was longing to meet you. May we sit down on this sofa and talk a little, or were you just starting for your drive?"

"Of course we may sit down," said Theodora. "My drive does not matter in the least. It was so good of you to come."

And her inward thought was that she would like Hector's sister. Anne's frankness and *sans gêne* were so pleasing.

They exchanged a few agreeable sentences while each measured the other, and then Lady Anningford said:

"You come from Australia, don't you?"

"Australia!" smiled Theodora, while her eyes opened wide. "Oh no! I have never been out of France and Belgium and places like that. My husband lived in Melbourne for some years, though."

"I thought it could not be possible," quoth Anne to herself.

"Then you don't know much of England yet?" she said, aloud.

"It is my first visit; and it seems very dull and rainy. This is the only really fine day we have had since we arrived."

Anne soon dexterously elicited an outline of Theodora's plans and what she was doing. They would only remain in town until Whitsuntide, perhaps returning later for a week or two; and Mrs. Devlyn, to whom her father had sent her an introduction, had been kind enough to tell them what to do and how to see a little of London. She was going to a ball to-night. The first real ball she had ever been to in her life, she said, ingenuously.

And Lady Anningford looked at her and each moment fell more under her charm.

"The ball at Harrowfield House, I expect, to meet the King of Guatemala," she said, knowing Lady Harrowfield was Florence Devlyn's cousin.

"That is it," said Theodora.

"Then you must dance with Hector—my brother," she said.

She launched his name suddenly; she wanted to see what effect it would have on Theodora. "He is sure to be there, and he dances divinely."

She was rewarded for her thrust: just the faintest pink came into the white velvet cheeks, and the blue eyes melted softly. To dance with Hector! Ah! Then the radiance was replaced by a look of sadness, and she said, quietly:

"Oh, I do not think I shall dance at all. My husband is rather an invalid, and we shall only go in for a little while."

No, she must not dance with Hector. Those joys were not for her—she must not even think of it.

"How extraordinarily beautiful she is!" Anne thought, when presently, the visit ended, she found herself rolling along in her electric brougham towards the park. "And I feel I shall love her. I wonder what her Christian name is?"

Theodora had promised they would lunch in Charles Street with her the next day if her husband should be well enough after the ball. And Anne decided to collect as many nice people to meet them as she could in the time.

At the corner of Grosvenor Square she met an old friend, one Colonel Lowerby, commonly called the Crow, and stopped to pick him up and take him on with her.

He was the one person she wanted to talk to at this juncture. She had known him all her life, and was accustomed to prattle to him on all subjects. He was always safe, and gruff, and honest.

"I have just done something so interesting, Crow," she told him, as they went along towards Regent's Park, to which sylvan spot she had directed her chauffeur, to be more free to talk in peace to her companion. Some of her friends were capable of making scandals, even about the dear old Crow, she knew.

"And what have you done?" he asked.

"Of course you have heard the tale from Uncle Evermond, of Hector and the lady at Monte Carlo?"

He nodded.

"Well, there is not a word of truth in it; he is in love, though, with the most beautiful woman I have ever seen in my life—and I have just been to call upon her. And to-morrow you have got to come to lunch to meet her—and tell me what you think."

"Very well," said the Crow. "I was feeding elsewhere, but I always obey you. Continue your narrative."

"I want you to tell me what to do, and how I can help them."

"My dear child," said the Crow, sententiously, as was his habit, "help them to what? She is married, of course, or Hector would not be in love with her. Do you want to help them to part or to meet? or to go to heaven or to hell? or to spend what Monica Ellerwood calls 'a Saturday to Monday amid rural scenery,' which means both of those things one after the other!"

"Crow, dear, you are disagreeable," said Lady Anningford, "and I have a cold in my head and cannot compete with you in words to-day."

"Then say what you want, and I'll listen."

"Hector met them in Paris, it seems, and must have fallen wildly in love, because I have never seen him as he is now."

"How is he?—and who is 'them'?"

"Why, she and the husband, of course, and Hector is looking sad and distrait—and has really begun to feel at last."

"Serve him right!"

"Crow, you are insupportable! Can you not see I am serious and want your help?"

"Fire away, then, my good child, and explain matters. You are too vague!"

So she told him all she knew—which was little enough; but she was eloquent upon Theodora's beauty.

"She has the face of an angel," she ended her description with.

"Always mistrust 'em," interjected the Crow.

"Such a figure and the nicest manner, and she is in love with Hector, too, of course—because she could not possibly help herself—could she?—if he is being lovely to her."

"I have not your prejudiced eyes for him—though Hector certainly is a decent fellow enough to look at," allowed Colonel Lowerby. "But all this does not get to what you want to do for them."

"I want them to be happy."

"Permanently, or for the moment?"

"Both."

"An impossible combination, with these abominably inconsiderate marriage laws we suffer under in this country, my child."

"Then what ought I to do?"

"You can do nothing but accelerate or hinder matters for a little. If Hector is really in love, and the woman, too, they are bound to dree their weird, one way or the other, themselves. You will be doing the greatest kindness if you can keep them apart, and avoid a scandal if possible."

"My dear Crow, I have never heard of your being so thoroughly unsympathetic before."

"And I have never heard of Hector being really in love before, and with an angel, too—deuced dangerous folk at the best of times!"

"Then there are mother and Morella Winmarleigh to be counted with."

"Neither of them can see beyond their noses. Miss Winmarleigh is sure of him, she thinks—and your mother, too."

"No; mother has her doubts."

"They will both be anti?"

"Extremely anti."

"To get back to facts, then, your plan is to assist your brother to see this 'angel,' and smooth the path to the final catastrophe."

"You worry me, Crow. Why should there be a catastrophe?"

"Is she a young woman?"

"A mere baby. Certainly not more than twenty or so."

"Then it is inevitable, if the husband don't count. You have not described him yet."

"Because I have never seen him," said Lady Anningford. "Hector did say last night, though, that he was an impossible Australian millionaire."

"These people have a strong sense of personal rights—they are even blood-thirsty sometimes, and expect virtue in their women. If he had been just an English snob, the social bauble might have proved an immense eye-duster; but when you say Australian it gives me hope. He'll take her away, or break Hector's head, before things become too embarrassing."

"Crow, you are brutal."

"And a good thing, too. That is what we all want, a little more brutality. The whole of the blessed show here is being ruined with this sickly sentimentality. Flogging done away with; every silly nerve pandered to. By Jove! the next time we have to fight any country we shall have an anæsthetic served round with the rations to keep Tommy Atkins's delicate nerves from suffering from the consciousness of the slaughter he inflicts upon the enemy."

"Crow, you are violent."

"Yes, I am. I am sick of the whole thing. I would reintroduce prize-fighting and bear-baiting and gladiatorial shows to brace the nation up a bit. We'll get jammed full of rotten vices like those beastly foreigners soon."

"I did not bring you into Regent's Park to hear a tirade upon the nation's needs, Crow," Anne reminded him, smiling, "but to get your sympathy and advice upon this affair of Hector. You know you are the only person in the world I ever talk to about intimate things."

"Dear Queen Anne," he said, "I will always do what I can for you. But I tell you seriously, when a man like Hector loves a woman really, you might as well try to direct Niagara Falls as to turn him any way but the one he means to go."

"He wants me to be kind to her. Do you advise me just to let the thing drop, then?"

"No; be as kind as you like—only don't assist them to destruction."

"She goes into the country on Saturday for Whitsuntide, as we all do. Hector is going down to Bracondale alone."

"That looks desperate. I shall see Hector, and judge for myself."

"You must be sure to go to the ball at Harrowfield House to-night, then," Anne said. "They are both going. I say both because I know she is, and so, of course, Hector will be there too. I shall go, naturally, and then we can decide what we can do about it after we have seen them together."

And all this time Theodora was thinking how charming Anne was, and how kind, and that she felt a little happier because of her kindness. And, hard as it would be, she would not leave Josiah's side that night or dance with Hector.

And Hector was thinking—

"What is the good of anything in this wide world without her? I *must* see her. For good or ill, I cannot keep away."

He was deep in the toils of desire and passionate love for a woman belonging to someone else and out of his reach, and for whom he was hungry. Thus the primitive forces of nature were in violent activity, and his soul was having a hard fight.

It was the first time in his life that a woman had really mattered or had been impossible to obtain.

He had always looked upon them as delightful accessories: sport first, and woman, who was only another form of sport, second.

He had not neglected the obligations of his great position, but they came naturally to him as of the day's work. They were not real interests in his life. And when stripped of the veneer of civilization he was but a passionate, primitive creature, like numbers of others of his class and age.

While the elevation of Theodora's pure soul was an actual influence upon him, he had thought it would be possible—difficult, perhaps—but possible to obey her—to keep from troubling her—to regulate his passion into worship at a distance. But since then new influences had begun to work—prominent among them being jealousy.

To see her surrounded by others—who were men and would desire her, too—drove him mad.

Josiah was difficult enough to bear. The thought that he was her husband, and had the rights of this position, always turned him sick with raging disgust; but that was the law, and a law accepted since the beginning of time. These others were not of the law—they were the same as himself—and would all try to win her.

He had no fear of their succeeding, but, to watch them trying, and he himself unable to prevent them, was a thought he could not tolerate.

He had no settled plan. He did not deliberately say to himself: "I will possess her at all costs. I will be her lover, and take her by force from the bonds of this world." His whole mind was in a ferment and chaos. There was no time to think of the position in cold blood. His passion hurried him on from hour to hour.

This day after the opera, when the hideous impossibility of the situation had come upon him with full force, he felt as Lancelot—

"His mood was often like a fiend, and rose and drove him into wastes and solitudes for agony, Who was yet a living soul."

There are all sorts of loves in life, but when it is the real great passion, nor fear of hell nor hope of heaven can stem the tide—for long!

He had gone out in his automobile, and was racing ahead considerably above the speed limit. He felt he must do something. Had it been winter and hunting-time, he would have taken any fences—any risks. He returned and got to Ranelagh, and played a game of polo as hard as he could, and then he felt a little calmer. The idea came to him as it had done to Anne. Lady Harrowfield was Florence Devlyn's cousin; she would probably have squeezed an invitation for her protégées for the royal ball to-night. He would go—he must see Theodora. He must hold her in his arms, if only in the mazes of the waltz.

And the thought of that sent the blood whirling madly once more in his veins.

Everything he had looked upon so lightly up to now had taken a new significance in reference to Theodora. Florence Devlyn, for instance, was no fit companion for her—Florence Devlyn, whom he met at every decent house and had never before disapproved of, except as a bore and a sycophant.

XIX

Harrowfield House, as every one knows, is one of the finest in London; and with the worst manners, and an inordinate insolence, Lady Harrowfield ruled her section of society with a rod of iron. Indeed, all sections coveted the invitations of this disagreeable lady.

Her path was strewn with lovers, and protected by a proud and complacent husband, who had realized early he never would be master of the situation, and had preferred peace to open scandal.

She was a woman of sixty now, and, report said, still had her lapses. But every incident was carried off with a high-handed, brazen daring, and an assumption of right and might and prerogative which paralyzed criticism.

So it was that with the record of a *demimondaine*—and not one kind action to her credit—Lady Harrowfield still held her place among the spotless, and ruled as a queen.

There was not above two years' difference between her age and Lady Bracondale's; indeed, the latter had been one of her bridesmaids; but no one to look at them at a distance could have credited it for a minute.

Lady Harrowfield had golden hair and pink cheeks, and her *embonpoint* retained in the most fashionable outline. And if towards two in the morning, or when she lost at bridge, her face did remind on-lookers of a hideous colored mask of death and old age—one can't have everything in life; and Lady Harrowfield had already obtained more than the lion's share.

This night in June she stood at the top of her splendid staircase, blazing with jewels, receiving her guests, among whom more than one august personage, English and foreign, was expected to arrive; and an unusually sour frown disfigured the thick paint of her face.

It all seemed like fairy-land to Theodora as, accompanied by Josiah, and preceded by Mrs. Devlyn, she early mounted the marble steps with the rest of the throng.

She noticed the insolent stare of her hostess as she shook hands and then passed on in the crowd.

She felt a little shy and nervous and excited withal. Every one around seemed to have so many friends, and to be so gay and joyous, and only she and Josiah stood alone. For Mrs. Devlyn felt she had done enough for one night in bringing them there.

It was an immense crowd. At a smaller ball Theodora's exquisite beauty must have commanded instant attention, but this was a special occasion, and the world was too occupied with a desire to gape at the foreign king to trouble about any new-comers. Certainly for the first hour or so.

Josiah was feeling humiliated. Not a creature spoke to them, and they were hustled along like sheep into the ballroom.

A certain number of men stared—stared with deep interest, and made plans for introductions as soon as the crowd should subside a little.

Theodora was perfectly dressed, and her jewels caused envy in numbers of breasts.

She was too little occupied with herself to feel any of Josiah's humiliation. This society was hers by right of birth, and did not disconcert her; only no one could help being lonely when quite neglected, while others danced.

Presently, a thin, ill-tempered-looking old man made his way with difficulty up to their corner; he had been speaking to Mrs. Devlyn across the room.

"I must introduce myself," he said, graciously, to Theodora. "I am your uncle, Patrick Fitzgerald, and I am so delighted to meet you and make your acquaintance."

Theodora bowed without *empressement*. She had no feeling for these relations who had been so indifferent to her while she was poor and who had treated darling papa so badly.

"I only got back to town last night, or I and my wife would have called at Claridge's before this," he continued. And then he said something affable to Josiah, who looked strangely out of place among this brilliant throng.

For whatever may compose the elements of the highest London society, the atoms all acquire a certain air after a little, and if within this *fine fleur* of the aristocracy there lurked some Jews and Philistines and infidels of the middle classes, they were not quite new to the game, and had all received their gloss. So poor Josiah stood out rather by himself, and Sir Patrick Fitzgerald felt a good deal ashamed of him.

Theodora's fine senses had perceived all this long ago—the contrast her husband presented to the rest of the world—and it had made her stand closer to him and treat him with more deference than usual; her generous heart always responded to any one or anything in an unhappy position.

And through all his thick skin Josiah felt something of her tenderness, and glowed with pride in her.

Sir Patrick Fitzgerald continued to talk, and even paid his niece some bluff compliments. Her manner was so perfect, he decided! Gad! he could be proud of his new-found relation. And though the husband was nothing but a grocer still, and looked it every inch, by Jove, he was rich enough to gild his vulgarity and be tolerated among the highest.

Thus the uncle was gushing and lavish in his invitations and offers of friendship. They must come to Beechleigh for Whitsuntide. He would hear of no refusal. Going home! Oh, what nonsense! Home was a place one could go to at any time. And he would so like to show them Beechleigh at its best, where her father had lived all his young life.

Josiah was caught by his affable suggestions. Why should they not go? Only that morning he had received a letter from his agent at Bessington Hall to say the place, unfortunately, would not be completely ready for them. Why, then, should they not accept this pleasant invitation?

Theodora hesitated—but he cut her short.

"I am sure it is very good of you, Sir Patrick, and my wife and I will be delighted to come," he said.

By this time the excitement of the royal entrance and quadrille had somewhat subsided, and several people felt themselves drawn to be presented to the beautiful young woman in white with the really fine jewels, and before she knew where she was, Theodora found herself waltzing with a wonderfully groomed, ugly young marquis.

She had meant not to dance—not to leave her husband's side; but fate and Josiah had ordered otherwise.

"Not dance! What nonsense, my love! Go at once with his lordship," he had said, when Sir Patrick had presented Lord Wensleydown. And wincing at the sentence, Theodora had allowed herself to be whirled away.

Her partner was not more than nine-and-twenty; but he had all the blasé airs of a man of forty. He began to say *entreprenant* things to Theodora after three turns round the room.

She was far too unsophisticated to understand their ultimate meaning, but they made her uncomfortable.

He gazed at her loveliness with that insulting look of sensual admiration which some men think the highest compliment they can pay to a woman. And just in the middle of all this, Hector Bracondale arrived upon the scene. He had been searching for her everywhere; in that crowd one could miss any one with ease. He stood and watched her before she caught sight of him—watched her pure whiteness in the clutches of this beast of prey. Saw his burning looks; noted his attitude; imagined his whisperings—and murderous feelings leaped to his brain.

How dared Wensleydown! How dared any one! Ah, God! and he was powerless to prevent it. She was the wife of Josiah Brown over there, smiling and complacent to see *his* belonging dancing with a marquis!

"Hector, dearest, what is the matter?" exclaimed Lady Anningford, coming up at that moment to her brother's side. She was with Colonel Lowerby, and they had made a tour of the rooms on purpose to see Theodora. "You appear ready to murder some one. What has happened?"

Hector looked straight at her. She was a very tall woman, almost his height, and she saw pain and rage and passion were swimming in his eyes, while his deep voice vibrated as he answered:

"Yes, I want to murder some one—and possibly will before the evening is over."

"Hector! Crow, leave me with him, like the dear you always are," she whispered to Colonel Lowerby, "and come and find me again in a few minutes."

"Hector, what is it?" she asked, anxiously, when they stood alone.

"Look!" said Lord Bracondale. "Look at Wensleydown leaning over Theodora." He was so moved that he uttered the name without being aware of it. "Did you ever see such a damned cad as he is? Good God, I cannot bear it!"

"He—he is only dancing with her," said Anne, soothingly. What had come to her brother, her whimsical, cynical brother, who troubled not at all, as a rule, over anything in the world?

"Only dancing with her! I tell you I will not bear it. Where is the Crow? Why did you send him off? I can't stay with you; I must go and speak to her, and take her away from this."

"Hector, for Heaven's sake do not be so mad," said Lady Anningford, now really alarmed. "You can't go up and seize a woman from her partner in the middle of a waltz. You must be completely crazy! Dear boy, let us stay here by the door until the music finishes, and then I will speak to her before they can leave the room to sit out."

She put her hand on his arm to detain him, and started to feel how it trembled.

What passion was this? Surely the Crow was right, after all, and it could only lead to some inevitable catastrophe. Anne's heart sank; the lights and the splendor seemed all a gilded mockery.

At that moment Morella Winmarleigh advanced with Evermond Le Mesurier—their uncle Evermond—who, having other views for his own amusement, left her instantly at Anne's side and disappeared among the crowd.

"How impossible to find any one in this crush!" Miss Winmarleigh said. There was a cackly tone in her voice, especially when raised above the din of the music, which was peculiarly irritating to sensitive ears.

Hector felt he hated her.

Anne still kept her hand on his arm, and flight was hopeless.

Just then a Royalty passed with their hostess, and claimed Lady Anningford's attention, so Hector was left sole guardian of Morella Winmarleigh.

She cackled on about nothing, while his every sense was strained watching Theodora, to see that she did not leave the room without his knowledge.

She was whirling still in the maze of the waltz, and each time she passed fresh waves of rage surged in Hector's breast, as he perceived the way in which Lord Wensleydown held her.

"Why, there is the woman who was at the opera last night," exclaimed Morella, at last. "How in the world did an outsider like that get here, I wonder? She is quite pretty, close—don't you think so, Hector? Oh, I forgot, you know her, of course; you talked to her last night, I remember."

Hector did not answer; he was afraid to let himself speak.

Morella Winmarleigh was looking her best. A tonged, laced, flounced best; and she was perfectly conscious of it, and pleased with herself and her attractions.

She meant to keep Lord Bracondale with her for the rest of the evening if possible, even if she had to descend to tricks scarcely flattering to her own vanity.

"Do let us go for a walk," she said. "I have not yet seen the flower decorations in the yellow salon, and I hear they are particularly fine."

Hector by this time was beside himself at seeing Theodora converging with her partner towards the large doors at the other end of the ballroom.

"No," he said. "I am very sorry, but I am engaged for the next dance, and must go and hunt up my partner. Where can I take you?"

Hector engaged for a dance? An unknown thing, and of course untrue. What could this mean? Who would he dance with? That colonial creature? This must be looked into and stopped at once.

Miss Winmarleigh's thin under-lip contracted, and a deeper red suffused her blooming cheeks.

"I really don't know," she said. "I am quite lost, and I am afraid you can't leave me until I find some one to take care of me." And she giggled girlishly.

That such a large cow of a woman should want protection of any sort seemed quite ridiculous to Hector—maddeningly ridiculous at the present moment. Theodora had disappeared, having seen him standing there with Morella Winmarleigh, who she had been told he was going to marry.

He was literally white with suppressed rage. The Royalty had commandeered Anne, and among the dozens of people he knew there was not one in sight with whom he could plant Morella Winmarleigh; so he gave her his arm, and hurried along the way Theodora had disappeared.

"Are you going to Beechleigh for Whitsuntide?" Morella asked. "I am, and I think we shall have a delightful party."

Hector was not paying the least attention. Theodora was completely out of sight now, and might be lost altogether, for all they were likely to overtake her among this crowd and the numberless exits and entrances.

"Beechleigh!" he mumbled, absently. "Who lives there? I don't even know. I am going home."

"Why, Hector, of course you know! The Fitzgeralds—Sir Patrick and Lady Ada. Every one does."

Then it came to him. These were Theodora's uncle and aunt. Was it possible she could be going there, too? He recollected she had told him in Paris her father had written to this brother of his about her coming to London. She might be going. It was a chance, and he must ascertain at once.

Sir Patrick Fitzgerald he knew at the Turf, and now that he thought of it he knew Lady Ada by sight quite well, and he was aware he would be a welcome guest at any house. If Theodora was going, he expected the thing could be managed. Meanwhile, he must find her, and get rid of Morella Winmarleigh. He hurried her on through the blue salon and the yellow salon and out into the gallery beyond. Theodora had completely disappeared.

Miss Winmarleigh kept up a constant chatter of commonplaces, to which, when he replied at all, he gave random answers.

And every moment she became more annoyed and uneasy.

She had known Hector since she was a child. Their places adjoined in the country, and she saw him constantly when there. Her stolid vanity had never permitted the suggestion to come to her that he had always been completely indifferent to her. She intended to marry him. His mother shared her wishes. They were continually thrown together, and the thought of her as a probable ending to his life when all pleasures should be over had often entered his head.

Before he met Theodora, if he had ever analyzed his views about Morella, they probably would have been that she was a safe bore with a great many worldly advantages. A woman who you could be sure would not take a lover a few years after you had married her, and whom he would probably marry if she were still free when the time came.

His flittings from one pretty matron to another had not caused her grave anxieties. He could not marry them, and he never talked with girls or possible rivals. So she had always felt safe and certain that fate would ultimately make him her husband.

But this was different—he had never been like this before. And uneasiness grabbed at her well-regulated heart.

"Ah, there is my mother!" he exclaimed, at last, with such evident relief that Morella began to feel spiteful.

They made their way to where Lady Bracondale was standing. She beamed upon them like a pleased pussy-cat. It looked so suitable to see them thus together!

"Dearest," she said to Morella, "is not this a lovely ball? And I can see you are enjoying yourself."

Miss Winmarleigh replied suitably, and her stolid face betrayed none of her emotion.

"Mother," said Hector, "I wish you would introduce me to Lady Ada Fitzgerald when you get the chance. I see her over there."

This was so obvious that Morella, who never saw between the lines, preened with pleasure. After all, he wished to spend Whitsuntide with her, and this anxiety to find Lady Bracondale had been all on that account. Lady Bracondale, who was acquainted with Miss Winmarleigh's plans, made the same interruption, and joy warmed her being.

She was only too pleased to do whatever he wished. And the affair was soon accomplished.

Hector made himself especially attractive, and Lady Ada Fitzgerald decided he was charming.

The way paved for possible contingencies, he escaped from this crowd of women, and once more began his search for Theodora. She would certainly return to Josiah some time. To go straight to him would be the best plan.

Josiah was standing absolutely alone by one of the windows in the ballroom, and looked pitiably uncomfortable and ill at ease in his knee-breeches and silk stockings.

He had experienced such pleasure when he had tried them on, and had enjoyed walking through the hall at Claridge's to his carriage, knowing the people there would be aware it meant he was going to meet the most august Royalty.

But now he felt uncomfortable, and kept standing first on one leg, then on the other. Theodora had not returned to him yet: the next dance had not begun.

This great world contained discomfort as well as pleasure, he decided.

Hector walked straight over to him and was excessively polite and agreeable, and Josiah's equanimity was somewhat restored.

What could have happened to Theodora? Where had that beast Wensleydown taken her? Not to supper—surely not to supper?—were Lord Bracondale's thoughts.

And then with the first notes of the next dance she reappeared. It seemed to him she was looking superbly lovely: a faint pink suffused her cheeks, and her eyes were shining with the excitement of the scene.

A mad rush of passion surged over Hector; his turn had come, he thought.

Lord Wensleydown seemed loath to release her, and showed signs of staying to talk awhile. So Hector interposed at once.

"May I not have this dance? I have been looking for you everywhere," he said.

Theodora told him she was tired, and she stood close to her husband; tired—and also she was quite sure Josiah would be bored left all alone, so she wished to stay with him.

But Mrs. Devlyn made a reappearance just then, and as they spoke they saw Josiah give her his arm and lead her away.

Thus Theodora was left standing alone with Lord Bracondale.

Fate seemed always to nullify her good intentions.

It was an exquisite waltz, and the music mounted to both their brains.

For one moment the room appeared to reel in front of her, and then she found herself whirling in his arms. Oh, what bliss it was, after this long week of separation! What folly and maddening bliss!

Her senses were tingling; her lithe, exquisite, willowy body thrilled and quivered in his embrace. And they both realized what a waltz could be, as a medium for joy.

"We will only have two turns until the crowd gets impossible again," he whispered, "and then I will take you to supper."

Lady Anningford had been rejoined by the Crow, and now stood watching them. She and her companion were silent for a moment, and then:

"By Jove!" Colonel Lowerby said. "She is certainly worth going to hell for, to look at even—and they don't appear as if they would take long on the road."

XX

"Oh, Crow, dear, what are we to do, then?" said Lady Anningford. "Surely, surely you don't anticipate any sudden catastrophe? In these days people never run away—"

"No," said the Crow. "They stay at home until the footman, or the man's last mistress, or the woman's dearest friend, send anonymous letters to the husband."

"But—"

"Well, I tell you, Queen Anne, to me this appears serious. I know Hector pretty well, and I have never seen him as far gone as this before. The woman—she is a mere child—looks as unsophisticated as a baby, and probably is. She won't have the least idea of managing the affair. She will tumble headlong into it."

"Well, what is to be done, then?" exclaimed Anne, piteously.

"You had better talk to him quietly. He is very fond of you. Though nothing, I am afraid, will be of the least use," said the Crow.

"But if she is going into the country they won't meet," reasoned Anne. "You saw the dreadful-looking husband just now. Will he be the colonial who will object, do you think, or the English snob who won't?"

But the Crow refused to give any more opinions except in general.

It all came, he said, from the ridiculous marriage laws in this over-civilized country. Why should not people eminently suited to each other be allowed to be happy?

"It is too bad, Crow," said Anne. "You take it for granted that Hector has the most dishonorable intentions towards Mrs. Brown. He may worship her quite in the abstract."

"Fiddle-dee-dee, my child!" said Colonel Lowerby. "Look at him! You don't understand the fundamental principles of human nature if you say that. When a man is madly in love with a woman, nature says, 'This is your mate,' not a saint of alabaster on a church altar. There are numbers of animals about who find a 'mate' in every woman they come across. But Hector is not that sort. Look at his face—look at him now they are passing us, and tell me if you see any abstract about it?"

Anne was forced to admit she did not; and it was with intense uneasiness she saw her brother and his partner stop, and disappear through one of the doors towards the supper-room.

When her mother perceived the situation—or Morella—disagreeable moments would begin at once for everybody!

Meanwhile, the culprits were extremely happy.

With the finest and noblest intention in the world, Theodora was too young, and too healthy, not to have become exhilarated with the dance and the scene. Something whispered, Why should she not enjoy herself to-night? What harm could there be in dancing? Every one danced—and Josiah, himself, had left her alone.

Hector had not said a word that she must rebuke him for; they had just waltzed and thrilled, and been—happy!

And now she was going to eat some supper with him, and forget there were any to-morrows.

They found a secluded corner, and spent half an hour in perfect peace. Hector was an artist in pleasing women—and to-night, though he never once transgressed in words, she could feel through it all that he loved her—loved her madly. His voice was so tender and deep, and his thought for her slightest wish and comfort so evident; he was masterful, too, and settled what she was to do—where to sit, and now and then he made her look at him.

He was just so wildly happy he could not stop to count the cost; and while he worshipped her more deeply than when they had sat on the soft greensward at Versailles, even the whole sight of her pure soul now could not stop him—now he knew she loved him, and that there were possible others on the scene. She had trusted him—had appealed to his superior strength; he did not forget that fact quite—but here at a ball was not the place to analyze what it would mean. They were just two guests dancing and supping like the rest, and were supremely content.

He found out where she was going for Whitsuntide, but said nothing of his own intentions.

The blindness and madness of love was upon him and held him in complete bondage. The first shock, which her look of the wounded fawn had given him, was over. They had suffered, and made good resolutions, and parted, and now they had met again. And he could not, and would not, think where they might drift to.

To be near her, to look into her eyes, to be conscious of her personality was what he asked at the moment, what he must have. The rest of time was a blank, and meaningless. It is not every man who loves in this way—fortunately for the rest of the world! Many go through life with now and then a different woman merely as an episode, as far as anything but a physical emotion is concerned. Sport, or their own ambitions, fill up their real interests, and no woman could break their hearts.

But Hector was not of these. And this woman had it in her power to make his heaven or hell.

They had both passed through moments of exalted sentiment, even a little dramatic in their tragedy and renunciation, but circumstance is stronger always than any highly strung emotion of good or evil. At the end of their good-bye at Madrid their story should have closed, as the stories in books so often do, with the hero and heroine worked up to some wonderful pitch of self-sacrifice and drama. They so seldom tell of the flatness of the afterwards. The impossibility of retaining a balance on this high pinnacle of moral valor, where circumstance, which is a commonplace and often material thing, decrees that the lights shall not be turned out with the ring-down of the curtain.

Unless death finishes what is apparently the last act, there is always the tomorrow to be reckoned with—out of the story-book. So while exalted—he by his sudden worship of that pure sweetness of soul in Theodora which he had discovered, she by her innocence and desire to do right—they had been able to tune their minds to an idea of a tender good-bye, full of sentiment and vows of abstract devotion, and adherence to duty.

And if he had gone to the ends of the earth that night the exaltation, as a memory, might have continued, and time might have healed their hurts—time and the starvation of absence and separation. But fate had decreed they should meet again, and soon; and all the forces which precipitate matters should be employed for their undoing.

For all else in life Hector was no weakling. He had always been a strong man, physically and morally.

His views were the views of the world. It seemed no great sin to him to love another man's wife. All his friends did the same at one period or another.

It was only when Theodora had awakened him that he had begun even to think of controlling himself.

It was to please her, not because he was really convinced of the right and necessity of their course of action, that he had said good-bye and agreed to worship her in the abstract.

He had been highly moved and elevated by her that night in Paris. And when he wrote the letter his honest intention had been to follow its words.

He did not recognize the fact that without the zeal of blind faith as to the right, human nature must always yield to inclination.

So they sat there and ate their supper, and forgot to-morrow, and were radiantly happy.

As they had gone down the stairs Monica Ellerwood had joined Lady Bracondale in the gallery above.

"Oh! Look, Aunt Milly!" she had said. "Hector is with the American I told you about in Paris. Do you see, going down to supper. Oh, isn't she pretty! and what jewels—look!"

And Lady Bracondale had moved forward in a manner quite foreign to her usual dignity to catch sight of them.

"It is the same woman he talked to at the opera last night," she said. "She is not an American, but a Mrs. Brown, an Australian millionaire's wife, we were told. She is certainly pretty. Oh—eh—you said Hector was devoted to her in Paris?"

"Why, of course! You can ask Jack."

"I do not think we need worry, though, dear, because I am happy to say Hector shows great signs of wishing to be with Morella."

And with this pleasing thought she had turned the conversation.

"I think we must go back now," said Theodora, after she had finished the last monster strawberry on her plate. "Josiah may be waiting for me."

Oh, she had been so happy! There was that sense vibrating through everything that he loved her, and they were together—but now it must end.

So they made their way up the stairs and back to the ballroom.

Mrs. Devlyn had abandoned Josiah, and he stood once more alone and supremely uncomfortable. A pang of remorse seized Theodora; she wished she had not stayed so long; she would not leave him again for a moment.

He had supped, it appeared, been hurried over it because Mrs. Devlyn wished to return, and was now feeling cross and tired. He was quite ready to leave when Theodora suggested it, and they said good-night to Hector and descended to find their carriage. But in that crowd it was not such an easy matter.

There was a long wait in the hall, where they were joined by the assiduous Marquis and Delaval Stirling. And Hector, from a place on the stairs, had all his feelings of jealous rage aroused again in watching them while he was detained where he was by his hostess.

Meanwhile, Sir Patrick Fitzgerald had gone about telling every one of the beauty of his new-found niece, and had brought his wife to be introduced to her just after Theodora had left.

Since his scapegrace brother was going to make such an advantageous marriage, and this niece had proved a lovely woman, and rich withal, he quite admitted the ties of blood were thicker than water.

Lady Ada was not of like opinion; she had enough relations of her own, and resented his having asked the Browns to Beechleigh for Whitsuntide.

"My party was all made up but for one extra man," she said, "whom I think I have found; and we did not need these people."

XXI

Lord Bracondale arrived at his sister's house in Charles Street about a quarter of an hour before her luncheon guests were due.

Anne rushed down to see him, meeting her husband on the stairs.

"Oh, don't come in yet, Billy, like a darling," she said, "I want to talk to Hector alone."

And the meek and fond Lord Anningford had obediently retired to his smoking-room.

"Well, Hector," she said, when she had greeted him, "and so you are going to the Fitzgeralds' for Whitsuntide, and not to Bracondale, mother tells me this morning. She is in the seventh heaven, taking it for a sign, as you had to manœuvre so to be asked, that things are coming to a climax between you and Morella."

"Morella? Is she going?" said Hector, absently. He had quite forgotten that fact, so perfectly indifferent was he to her movements, and so completely had his own aims engrossed him.

"Why—dear boy!" Anne gasped. The whole scene, highly colored by repetition, had been recounted to her. How Morella had told him of her plans, and how he had at once got introduced to Lady Ada, and played his cards so skilfully that the end of the evening produced the invitation.

"Oh yes, of course, I remember she is going," he said, impatiently. "Anne, you haven't asked that beast Wensleydown to-day, have you?"

"No, dear. What made you think so?"

"I saw you talking to him in the park this morning, and I feared you might have. I shall certainly quarrel with him one of these days."

"You will have an opportunity, then, at Beechleigh, as he will be there. He is always with the Fitzgeralds," Anne said, and she tried to laugh. "But don't make a scandal, Hector."

She saw his eyes blaze.

"He is going there, is he?" he said, and then he stared out of the window.

Anne knew nothing of the relationship between Theodora and Sir Patrick. She never for a moment imagined the humble Browns would be invited to this exceptionally smart party. And yet she was uneasy. Why was Hector going? What plan was in his head? Not Morella, evidently. But she had never believed that would be his attraction.

And Hector was too preoccupied to enlighten her.

"Is mother coming to lunch?" he asked.

"Yes, by her own request. I had not meant to ask her—Oh, well, you know, she is never very pleased at your having new friends, and I thought she might fix Mrs. Brown with that stony stare she has sometimes, and we would be happier without her; but she was determined to come."

"It is just as well," he said, "because she will have to get accustomed to it. I shall ask my friends the Browns down to Bracondale on every occasion, and as she is hostess there the stony stare won't answer."

"Manage her as best you may," said Anne. "But you know how she can be now and then—perfectly annihilating to unfortunate strangers."

Hector's finely chiselled lips shut like a vise.

"We shall see," he said. "And who else have you got? None of the Harrowfield-Devlyn crew, I hope—"

"Hector, how strange you are! I thought you and Lady Harrowfield were the greatest friends, so of course I asked her. No one in London can make a woman's success as she can."

"Or mar it so completely if she takes a dislike! Have you ever heard of her doing a kindness to any one? I haven't!" he said, irritably.

Then he walked to the window and back quickly.

"I tell you I am sick of it all, Anne. Last night, whoever I spoke to had something vile to impute or insinuate about every one they mentioned; and Lady Harrowfield, with a record of her own worse than the lowest, rode a high horse of virtue, and was more spiteful than all the rest put together. I loathe them, the whole crew. What do they know of anything good or pure or fine? Painted Jezebels, the lot of them!"

"Hector!" almost screamed Lady Anningford. "What has come over you, my dear boy?"

"I will tell you," he said; and his voice, which had been full of passion, now melted into a tone of deep tenderness. "I love a woman whose pure goodness has taught me there are other possibilities in life beyond the aims of these vile harpies of our world—a woman whose very presence makes one long to be better and nobler, whose dear soul has not room for anything but kind and loving thoughts of sweetness and light. Oh, Anne, if I might have her for my own, and live away down at Bracondale far from all this, I think—I think I, too, could learn what heaven would mean on earth."

"Dear Hector!" said Anne, who was greatly moved. "Oh, I am so sorry for you! But what is to be done? She is married to somebody else, and you will only injure her and yourself if you see too much of her."

"I know," he said. "I realize it sometimes—this morning, for instance—and then—and then—"

He did not add that the thought of Lord Wensleydown and the rest swarming round Theodora drove him mad, deprived him of his power of reasoning, and filled him with a wild desire to protect her, to be near her, to keep her always for himself, always in his sight.

"Anne," he said, at last, "promise me you will go out of your way to be kind to her. Don't let these other odious women put pin-points into her, because she is so innocent, and all unused to this society. She is just my queen and my darling. Will you remember that?"

And as Anne looked she saw there were two great tears in his eyes—his deep-gray eyes which always wore a smile of whimsical mockery—and she felt a lump in her throat.

This dear, dear brother! And she could do nothing to comfort him—one way or another.

"Hector, I will promise—always," she said, and her voice trembled. "I am sure she is sweet and good; and she is so lovely and fascinating—and oh, I wish—I wish—too!"

Then he bent down and kissed her, just as his mother and Lady Harrowfield came into the room.

Anne felt glad she had not informed them they were to meet the Browns, as was her first intention. She seemed suddenly to see with Hector's eyes, and to realize how narrow and spiteful Lady Harrowfield could be.

Most of the guests arrived one after the other, and were talking about the intimate things they all knew, when "Mr. and Mrs. Brown" were announced, and the whole party turned to look at them, while Lady Harrowfield tittered, and whispered almost audibly to her neighbor:

"These are the creatures Florence insisted upon my giving an invitation to last night. I did it for her sake, of course, so wretchedly poor she is, dear Florence, and she hopes to make a good thing out of them. Look at the man!" she added. "Has one ever sees such a person, except in a pork-butcher's shop!"

"I have never been in one," said Hector, agreeably, a dangerous flash in his eyes; "but I hear things are too wonderfully managed at Harrowfield

House—though I had no idea you did the shopping yourself, dear Lady Harrowfield."

She looked up at him, rage in her heart. Hector had long been a hopeless passion of hers—so good-looking, so whimsical, and, above all, so indifferent! She had never been able to dominate and ride rough-shod ever him. When she was rude and spiteful he answered her back, and then neglected her for the rest of the evening.

But why should he defend these people, whom, probably, he did not even know?

She would watch and see.

Then they went in to luncheon, without waiting for two or three stray young men who were always late.

And Theodora found herself sitting between the Crow and a sleek-looking politician; while poor Josiah, extremely ill at ease, sat at the left hand of his hostess.

Anne had purposely not put Hector near Theodora; with her mother there she thought it was wiser not to run any risks.

Lady Bracondale was sufficiently soothed by her happy dream of the cause of Hector's visit to Beechleigh to be coldly polite to Theodora, whom Anne had presented to her before luncheon. She sat at the turn of the long, oval table just one off, and was consequently able to observe her very carefully.

"She is extremely pretty and looks well bred—quite too extraordinary," she said to herself, in a running commentary. "Grandfather a convict, no doubt. She reminds me of poor Minnie Borringdon, who ran off with that charming scapegrace brother of Patrick Fitzgerald. I wonder what became of them?"

Lady Bracondale deplored the ways of many of the set she was obliged to move in—Delicia Harrowfield, for instance. But what was one to do? One must know one's old friends, especially those to whom one had been a bridesmaid!

The Crow, who had begun by being determined to find Theodora as cunning as other angels he was acquainted with, before the second course had fallen completely under her spell.

No one to look into her tender eyes could form an adverse opinion about her; and her gentle voice, which only said kind things, was pleasing to the ear.

"'Pon my soul, Hector is not such a fool as I thought," Colonel Lowerby said to himself. "This seems a bit of pure gold—poor little white lady! What will be the end of her?"

And opposite, Hector, with great caution, devoured her with his eyes.

Theodora herself was quite happy, though her delicate intuition told her Lady Harrowfield was antagonistic to her, and Hector's mother exceedingly stiff, while most of the other women eyed her clothes and talked over her head. But they all seemed of very little consequence to her, somehow.

She was like the sun, who continues to shine and give warmth and light no matter how much ugly imps may look up and make faces at him.

Theodora was never ill at ease. It would grieve her sensitive heart to the core if those she loved made the faintest shade of difference in their treatment of her—but strangers! They counted not at all, she had too little vanity.

Both her neighbors, the young politician and the Crow, were completely fascinated by her. She had not the slightest accent in speaking English, but now and then her phrasing had a quaint turn which was original and attractive.

Anne was not enjoying her luncheon-party. The impression of sorrow and calamity which the conversation with her brother had left upon her deepened rather than wore off.

Josiah's commonplace and sometimes impossible remarks perhaps helped it.

She seemed to realize how it must all jar on Hector. To know his loved one belonged to this worthy grocer—to understand the hopelessness of the position!

Anne was proud of her family and her old name. It was grief, too, to think that after Hector the title would go to Evermond Le Mesurier, the unmarried and dissolute uncle, if he survived his nephew, and then would die out altogether. There would be no more Baron Bracondales of Bracondale, unless Hector chose to marry and have sons. Oh, life was a topsy-turvy affair at the best of times, she sighed to herself.

Just before the ladies left the table, Josiah had announced their intended visit to Beechleigh, and his wife's relationship to Sir Patrick Fitzgerald and the old Earl Borringdon.

It came as a thunderclap to Lady Anningford. This accounted for Hector's eagerness to obtain the invitation—accounted for Theodora's exceeding look of breeding—accounted for many things.

She only trusted her mother had not heard the news also. So much better to leave her in her fool's paradise about Morella.

If Lady Harrowfield knew, she said nothing about it. She absolutely ignored Theodora, as though she had never shaken hands with her in her own house the night before. Theodora wondered at her manners—she did not yet know Mayfair.

The conversation turned upon some of the wonderful charities they were all interested in, and Theodora thought how good and kind of them to help the poor and crippled. And she said some gentle, sympathetic things to a lady who was near her. And Anne thought to herself how sweet and beautiful her nature must be, and it made her sadder and sadder.

Presently they all began to discuss the ball at Harrowfield House. It had been too lovely, they said, and Lady Harrowfield joined in with one of her sharp thrusts.

"Of course it could not be just as one would have wished. I was obliged to ask all sorts of people I had never even heard of," she said. "The usual grabbing for invitations, you know, to see the Royalties. Really, the quaint creatures who came up the stairs! I almost laughed in their faces once or twice."

"But don't you like to feel what pleasure you gave them, the poor things?" Theodora said, quite simply, without the least sarcasm. "You see, I know you gave them pleasure, because my husband and I were some of them—and we enjoyed it, oh, so much!"

And she smiled one of her adorable smiles which melted the heart of every one else in the room. But of Lady Harrowfield she made an enemy for life. The venomous woman reddened violently—under her paint—while she looked this upstart through and through. But Theodora was quite unconscious of her anger. To her Lady Harrowfield seemed a poor, soured old woman very much painted and ridiculous, and she felt sorry for unlovely old age and ill-temper.

Meanwhile, Lady Bracondale was being favorably impressed. She was a most presentable young person, this wife of the Australian millionaire, she decided.

Anne took the greatest pains to be charming to Theodora. They were sitting together on a sofa when the men came into the room.

Hector could keep away no longer. He joined them in their corner, while his face beamed with joy to see the two people he loved best in the world apparently getting on so well together.

"What have you been talking about?" he asked.

"Nothing very learned," said Anne. "Only the children. I was telling Mrs. Brown how Fordy's pony ran away in the park this morning, and how plucky he had been about it."

"They are rather nice infants," said Hector. "I should like you to see them," and he looked at Theodora. "Mayn't we have them down, Anne?"

Lady Anningford adored her offspring, and was only too pleased to show them; but she said:

"Oh, wait a moment, Hector, until some of these people have gone. Lady Harrowfield hates children, and Fordy made some terrible remarks about her wig last time."

"I wish he would do it again," said Hector. "She took the skin off every one the whole way through lunch."

"But Colonel Lowerby told me she was one of the cleverest women in London!" exclaimed Theodora; "and surely it is not very clever just to be bitter and spiteful!"

"Yes, she is clever," said Anne, with a peculiar smile, "and we are all rather under her thumb."

"It is perfectly ridiculous how you pander to her!" Hector said, impatiently. "I should never allow my wife to have anything but a distant acquaintance with her if I were married," and he glanced at Theodora.

Lady Anningford's duties as hostess took her away from them then, and he sat down on the sofa in her place.

"Oh, how I hate all this!" he said. "How different it is to Paris! It grates and jars and brings out the worst in one. These odious women and their little, narrow ways! You will never stay much in London—will you, Theodora?"

"I have always to do what Josiah wishes, you know; he rather likes it, and means us to come back after Whitsuntide, I think."

Hector seemed to have lost the power of looking ahead. Whitsuntide, and to be with her in the country for that time, appeared to him the boundary of his outlook.

What would happen after Whitsuntide? Who could say?

He longed to tell her how his thoughts were forever going back to the day at Versailles, and the peace and beauty of those woods—how all seemed here as though something were dragging him down to the commonplace, away out of their exalted dream, to a dull earth. But he dared not—he must keep to subjects less moving. So there was silence for some moments.

Theodora, since coming to London, had begun to understand it was possible for beautiful Englishmen to be husbands now and then, and that the term is not necessarily synonymous with "bore" and "duty"—as she had always thought it from her meagre experience.

She could not help picturing what a position of exquisite happiness some nice girl might have—some day—as Hector's wife. And she looked out of the window, and her eyes were sad. While the vision which floated to him at the same moment was of her at his side at Bracondale, and the delicious joy of possessing for their own some gay and merry babies like Fordy and his little brother and sister. And each saw a wistful longing in the other's eyes, and they talked quickly of banal things.

XXII

The Crow stayed on after all the other guests had left. He knew his hostess wished to talk to him.

It had begun to pour with rain, and the dripping streets held out no inducement to them to go out.

They pulled up their two comfortable arm-chairs to the sparkling wood fire, and then Colonel Lowerby said:

"You look sad, Queen Anne. Tell me about it."

"Yes, I am sad," said Anne. "The position is so hopeless. Hector loves her—loves her really—and I do not wonder at it; and she seems just everything that one could wish for him. A thousand times above Morella in intellect and understanding. All the things Hector and I like she sees at once. No need of explaining to her, as one has to to mother and Morella always."

"Yes," said the Crow. He did not argue with her as usual.

"It seems so fearful to think of her forever bound to that dreadful old grocer, whom she treats with so much deference and gentleness. The whole thing has made me sad. Hector is perfectly miserable; and, do you know, they are going to Beechleigh for Whitsuntide. Sir Patrick Fitzgerald is her uncle—and, of course, Hector is going, too, and—"

She did not finish her sentence. Her voice died away in a pathetic note as she gazed into the fire.

The Crow fidgeted; he had been devoted to Anne since she was a child of ten, and he hated to see her troubled.

"Look here," he said. "I investigated her thoroughly at luncheon, and I don't often make a mistake, do I?"

"No," said Anne. "Well—?"

"Well, she appeared to me to have some particular quality of sweetness—you were right about her looking like an angel—and I think she has got an angel's nature more or less; and when people are really like that there is some one up above looks after them, and I don't think we need worry much—you and I."

"Dear old Crow!" said Anne; "you do comfort me. But all the same, angel or not, Hector is so attractive—and he is a man, you know, not one of these anæmic, artistic, æsthetic things we see about so often now; and thrown together like that—how on earth will they be able to help themselves?"

The Crow was silent.

"You see," she continued, "beyond Morella, who is too absolutely unalluring and respectable to come to harm anywhere, and Miss Linwood, who only cares for bridge, there will hardly be another woman in the house who has not got a lover, and the atmosphere of those things is catching—don't you think so?"

"It is nature," said Colonel Lowerby. "A woman in possession of her health and faculties requires a mate, and when her husband is attending to sport or some other man's wife, she is bound to find one somewhere. I don't blame the poor things."

"Oh, nor I!" said Anne. "I don't ever blame any one. And just one, because you love him, seems all right, perhaps. It is six different ones in a year, and a seventh to pay the bills, that I find vulgar."

"Dans les premières passions, les femmes aiment l'amant; et dans les autres, elles aiment l'amour," quoted the Crow. "It was ever the same, you see. It is the seventh to pay the bills that seems vulgar and modern."

"Billy and I stayed there for the pheasant shoot last November, and I assure you we felt quite out of it, having no little adventures at night like the rest. Lady Ada is the picture of washed-out respectability herself, and so—to give her some reflected color, I suppose—she asks always the most go-ahead, advanced section of her acquaintances."

"Well, I shall be there this time," said the Crow; "she invited me last week."

This piece of news comforted Lady Anningford greatly. She felt here would be some one to help matters if he could.

"Morella will be perfectly furious when she gets there and finds she was not the reason of Hector's empressement for the invitation. And in her stolid way she can be just as spiteful as Lady Harrowfield."

"Yes, I know."

Then they were both silent for a while—Anne's thoughts busy with the mournful idea of the end of the House of Bracondale should Hector never marry, and the Crow's of her in sympathy, his eyes watching her face.

At last she spoke.

"I believe it would be best for Hector to go right away for a year or so," she sighed. "But, however it may be, I fear, alas! it can only end in tears."

XXIII

Beechleigh was really a fine place, built by Vanbrugh in his best days.

Three tiers of fifteen tall windows looked to the north in a front and two short wings, while colonnades led down to splendid wrought-iron gates, and blocks of buildings constructed in the same stately style. Fifteen more windows faced the south; and the centre one of the first floor led, with sweeping steps, to a terrace, while seven casements adorned each of the eastern and western sides.

On the southern side the view, for that rather flat country, was superb.

It gave, from a considerable elevation—through a wide opening of giant oaks and elms—a peep of the lake a mile below, and on in a long avenue of turf to a vista of smiling country.

On the splendid terrace peacocks spread their tails, and vases of carved stone broke at intervals the gray old balustrade.

Inside the house was equally nobly planned: all the rooms of great height and perfect proportion, and filled with pictures and tapestries and bronzes and antiques of immense value.

It had come to these spendthrift Irish Fitzgeralds through their grandmother, the last of an old ducal race. And two generations of Hibernian influence had curtailed the fine fortune which went with it, until Sir Patrick often felt it no easy matter to make both ends meet in the luxurious and gilded fashion which was necessary to himself and his friends.

If he and Lady Ada pinched and scraped when alone, keeping few servants on board wages, the parties, at all events, were done with all their wonted regal splendor.

"I shall stay with you, Patrick, as long as you can afford this cook," Lady Harrowfield said once to him; "but when you begin to economize, don't trouble to ask me. I hate poor people, when it shows."

A promising son, on the true Fitzgerald lines, was at Oxford now, and gave many anxious crows'-feet full opportunity of developing round his mother's faded eyes.

A plain daughter, Barbara, was pushed into corners and left much to herself. And a brilliant, flashing, up-to-date niece of Lady Ada's took always the first place.

Mildred was so clever, and her lovers were so well chosen, and so thoroughly of the right set or of great wealth; while a puny husband was helped to something in South Africa, when the man in possession was a Jew—or as agent for tea and jam in the colonies—when he happened to be only a colossally successful Englishman. And once, during a prominent politician's reign, poor Willie Verner enjoyed a few months in his own land as secretary to a newly started Radical club.

This Whitsuntide party was perhaps the smartest of the year.

By Saturday evening over thirty people would be gathered together under the Beechleigh roof.

Josiah, though exceedingly proud and pleased at the invitation, felt nervous at the thought of the visit. Not so Mr. Toplington, who, although he knew he should probably have to blush for his master, and might get a very secondary place in the "room," still felt he would hold his own when he could let it be known what magnificent wages he received from Mr. Brown.

"A long sight more than I'd get out of any lord," he thought. "And money is money. And all classes feels it."

Theodora, on the contrary, was neither proud nor pleased. She looked forward to the visit with excitement and dread.

Hector would be there, among all these people whom she did not know. And her awakened heart had begun to tell her that she loved him wildly, and to see him could only be alternate mad joy and remorse and anguish.

It was still drizzling on the Saturday afternoon when they arrived. So tea awaited them in the great saloon which made the centre of the north side of the house. Several of the rest of the guests had come down in the same train, but they did not know them, nor did any of them trouble themselves much to speak to them on the short drive from the station. A few words, that was all, addressed to Theodora. Josiah was ignored.

Sir Patrick had always been an excellent host. His genial Irish smile, when in action, concealed the ill-tempered lines of his thin old face. He greeted his guests cordially, and made them welcome to his home.

Lady Ada had the inherited bad manners of her family, the De Baronsvilles, who had come over with the Conqueror, and when one has a *cachet* like that there is no need to trouble one's self further. Thus, while Mildred flashed brilliant witticisms about, plain Barbara saw after the guests' tea and sugar, and if they took cream or lemon, and tiresome things like that. And as every one knew every one else, and the same party met continuously all over England, things were very gay and friendly.

Only Theodora and Josiah were completely out of it all, and several of the guests, who resented the intrusion of these strangers into their charmed circle, would take care on every opportunity to make them feel it.

Hector did not get there until half an hour later, in his automobile, which was the mode of arrival with more than two-thirds of the company.

And until the dressing-gong sounded, a continuous teuf-teuf-teuf might have been heard as, one after another, the cars whizzed up to the door.

Of course, in a troop of over thirty people, naturally some had kind hearts and good manners, but the prevailing tone of this coterie of *crème de la crème* was one of pure selfishness and blunt and material brutality.

If you were rich and suited them, you were given a nickname probably, and were allowed to play cards with them, and lose your money for their benefit. If you were non-congenial you did not exist—that was all. You might be sitting in a chair, but they only saw it and an empty space—you did not even cumber their ground.

To do them justice, they preferred people of their own exalted station; outsiders seldom made their way into this holy of holies, however rich they were—unless, of course, they happened to be Mildred's lovers. That situation for a man held special prerogatives, and was greatly coveted by pretenders to this circle of grace.

Intellectual intelligence was not important. Some of the women of this select company had been described by an agricultural duke who had stayed there as having just enough sense to come in out of the rain.

Sir Patrick Fitzgerald occasionally departed from the strict limits of this set in the big parties—especially lately, when money was becoming scarcer, several financial friends who could put him on to good things had been included, the result being that Lady Harrowfield had not always shed the light of her countenance upon the festivities.

Lord Harrowfield drew most of his income from a great, populous manufacturing city in the north, so neither he nor his countess had need to smile at mere wealth.

And Lady Harrowfield had said, frankly, "Let me know if it is a utility party, Patrick, or for just ourselves, because if you are going to have these creatures I sha'n't come."

This time, however, she had not been so exigent. It happened to suit some other arrangements of hers to spend Whitsuntide at Beechleigh, so she consented to chaperon Morella Winmarleigh without asking for a list of the guests.

Hector had never conformed to any special set; he went here, there, and everywhere, and was welcomed by all. But somehow, until this occasion, Beechleigh had never seen him within its gates, although Lady Harrowfield had praised him, and Mildred had sighed for him in vain.

He saw the situation at a glance when he came into the saloon: Josiah and Theodora sitting together, neglected by every one but Barbara. They could not have been more than half an hour in the house, he knew, for he had found out when the trains got in.

Barbara was a good sort; he remembered now he had met her before somewhere. She had evidently taken to the new cousin; but Mildred had not.

Hitherto Mildred had been the undisputed and acknowledged beauty of every party, and she resented Theodora's presence because she was clever enough not to have any illusions upon the matter of their mutual looks. She saw Theodora was beautiful and young and charming, and had every advantage of perfect Paris clothes. Uncle Patrick had been a fool to ask her, and she must take measures to suppress her at once.

Sir Patrick, on the other hand, was very pleased with himself for having given the invitation. He had made inquiries, and found that Josiah was a man of great and solid wealth, with interests in several things which could be of particular use to himself, and he meant to obtain what he could out of him.

As for Theodora, no living man could do anything but admire her, and Sir Patrick was not an Irishman for nothing.

Hector behaved with tact; he did not at once fly to his darling, but presently she found him beside her. And the now habitual thrill ran over her when he came near.

He saw the sudden, convulsive clasp of her little hands together; he knew how he moved her, and it gave him joy.

The next batch of arrivals contained Lord Wensleydown, who showed no hesitation as to his desired destination in the saloon. He made a bee-line for Theodora, and took a low seat at her feet.

Hector, with more caution, was rather to one side. Rage surged up in him, although his common-sense told him as yet there was nothing he could openly object to in Wensleydown's behavior.

The little picture of these five people—Barbara engaging Josiah, and the two men vying with each other to please Theodora—was gall and wormwood to Mildred. Freddy Wensleydown had always been one of her most valued friends, and for Hector she had often felt she could experience a passion.

- 132 -

Lord Wensleydown had an immense *cachet*. He was exceedingly ugly and exceedingly smart, and was known to have quite specially attractive methods of his own in the art of pleasing beautiful ladies. He was always unfaithful, too, and they had to make particular efforts to retain him for even a week.

Hector knew him intimately, of course; they had been in the same house at Eton, and were comrades of many years' standing, and until Theodora's entrance upon the scene, Hector had always thought of him as a coarse, jolly beast of extremely good company and quaintness. But now! He had no words adequate in his vocabulary to express his opinion about him!

To Theodora he appeared an ugly little man, who reminded her of the statue of a satyr she knew in the Louvre. That was all!

At this juncture Lady Harrowfield, accompanied by Morella Winmarleigh, her lord, and one of her *âmes damnées*, a certain Captain Forester, appeared upon the scene.

Their entrance was the important one of the afternoon, and Lady Ada and Sir Patrick could not do enough to greet and make them welcome.

The saloon was so large and the screens so well arranged, that for the first few seconds neither of the ladies perceived the fact of Theodora's presence. But when it burst upon them, both experienced unpleasant sensations.

Lady Harrowfield's temper was bad in any case on account of the weather, and here, on her arrival, that she should find the impertinent upstart who had made her look foolish at the Anningford luncheon, was an extra straw.

Morella felt furious. It began to dawn upon her this might be Hector's reason in coming, not herself at all; and one of those slow, internal rages which she seldom indulged in began to creep in her veins.

Thus it was that poor Theodora, all unconscious of any evil, was already surrounded by three bitter enemies—Mildred, Lady Harrowfield, and Morella Winmarleigh. It did not look as though her Whitsuntide could be going to contain much joy.

It was a good deal after six o'clock by now. Bridge-tables had already appeared, and most of the company had commenced to play. Barbara saw the look in Mildred's eye as she came across, and, ignoring Theodora quite, tried to carry off Lord Wensleydown.

"You must come, Freddy," she said. "Lady Harrowfield wants to begin her rubber."

Barbara, knowing what this move meant, and blushing for her cousin's rudeness, nervously introduced Theodora to her.

"How d' do," said Mildred, staring over her head. "Don't detain Lord Wensleydown, please, because Lady Harrowfield hates to be kept waiting."

Theodora rose and smiled, while she said to Barbara: "I am rather tired. Mayn't I go to my room for a little rest before dinner?"

"Take him, Lady Mildred, do," said Hector; "we don't want him," and he laughed gayly. His beautiful, tender angel might be a match for these people after all. At any rate, he would be at her side to protect her from their claws.

Lord Wensleydown frowned. Mildred was being a damned nuisance, he said to himself, and he insisted upon accompanying Theodora to the bottom of the great staircase, which rose to magnificent galleries in the hall adjoining the saloon.

Sir Patrick had advanced and engaged Josiah in conversation.

He knew his guests' ways and how they would boycott him, and, with a serious question like those Australian shares on the *tapis*, he was not going to have Josiah insulted and ruffled just yet.

"Don't stay up-stairs all the time," Hector had managed to whisper, while Mildred and Lord Wensleydown stood arguing; "they are sure not to dine till nine; there are two hours before you need dress, and we can certainly find some nice sitting-room to talk in."

But Theodora, with immense self-denial, had answered: "No, I want to write a long letter to papa and my sisters. I won't come down again until dinner."

And he was forced to be content with the memory of her soft smile and the evident regret in her eyes.

XXIV

Theodora was greatly interested in Beechleigh. To her the home of her fathers was full of sentiment, and the thought that her grandfather had ruled there pleased her. How she would love and cherish it were it her home now! Every one of these fine things must have some memory.

Then the pictures of as far back as she could remember came to her, and she saw again their poor lodgings in the cheap foreign towns and their often scanty fare. And with a fresh burst of love and pride in him, she remembered her father's invariable cheerfulness—cheerfulness and gayety—in such poverty! And after he had been used to—this! For all the descriptions of Captain Fitzgerald had given her no idea of the reality.

Now she knew what love meant, and could realize her mother's story. Oh, she would have acted just in the same way, too.

Dominic had been forgiven by his brother after his first wife's death, and had come back to enjoy a short spell of peace and prosperity. And who could wonder that Lady Minnie Borringdon, in her first season, and full of romance, should fall headlong in love with his wonderfully handsome face, and be only too ready to run off with him from an angry and unreasonable parent! She was a spoiled and only child who had never been crossed. Then came that fatal Derby, and the final extinction of all sympathy with the scapegrace. The Fitzgeralds had done enough for him already, and Lord Borringdon had no intention of doing anything at all, so the married lovers crept away in high disgrace, and spent a few months of bliss in a southern town, where the sun shone and the food was cheap, and there poor, pretty Minnie died, leaving Theodora a few hours old.

And now at Beechleigh Theodora looked out of her window on the north side—the southern rooms were kept for greater than she—and from there she could see a vast stretch of park, with the deer cropping the fine turf, and the lions frowning while they supported the ducal coronet over the great gates at the end of the court-yard and colonnade.

It was truly a splendid inheritance, and she glowed with pride to think she was of this house.

So she wrote a long letter to her dear ones—her sisters at Dieppe, and papa, still in Paris, and even one to Mrs. McBride. And then she read until her maid came to dress her for dinner.

Her room was a large one, and numberless modern touches of comfort brought up-to-date the early Georgian furniture and the shabby silk hangings.

A room stamped with that something which the most luxurious apartments of the wealthiest millionaire can never acquire.

Josiah looked in upon her as she finished dressing. He was, he said, most pleased with everything, and if they were a little unused to such company, still nothing could be more cordial than Sir Patrick's treatment of him.

Meanwhile, on their way up to dress, Mildred had gone in to Morella's room, and the two had agreed that Mrs. Brown should be suppressed.

It was with extra displeasure Miss Winmarleigh had learned of Theodora's relationship to Sir Patrick, and that after all she could not be called a common colonial.

There was no question about the Fitzgerald and Borringdon families, unfortunately, while Morella's grandfather had been merely a coal merchant.

"I don't think she is so wonderfully pretty, do you, Mildred?" she said.

But Mildred was a clever woman, and could see with her eyes.

"Yes, I do," she answered. "Don't be such a fool as to delude yourself about that, Morella. She is perfectly lovely, and she has the most deevie Paris clothes, and Lord Bracondale is wildly in love with her."

"And apparently Freddy Wensleydown, too," snapped Morella, who was now boiling with rage.

"Well, she is not likely to enjoy herself here," said Mildred, with her vicious laugh, which showed all her splendid, sharp teeth, as she went off to dress, her head full of plans for the interloper's suppression.

First she must have a few words with Barbara. There must be none of her partisanship. Poor, timid Barbara would not dare to disobey her, she knew. That settled, she did not fear that she would be able to make Theodora suffer considerably during the five days she would be at Beechleigh.

Sir Patrick was busy with some new arrivals who had come while they were dressing, so not a soul spoke to Theodora or Josiah when they got down to the great, white drawing-room, from which immensely high mahogany doors opened into an anteroom hung with priceless tapestry and containing cabinets of rare china. From thence another set of splendid carved doors gave access to the dining-room.

Neither Lord Wensleydown or Hector was in the room at first, so there was no man even to talk to them. Lady Ada had not introduced them to any one. And there they stood: Josiah ill at ease and uncomfortable, and Theodora quite apparently unconscious of neglect, while she looked at a picture.

All the younger women were thinking to themselves: "Who are these people? We don't want any strangers here—poaching on our preserves. And what perfect clothes! and what pearls! Why on earth did Ada ask them?"

And soon the party was complete, and Theodora found herself going in to dinner with her cousin Pat, who arrived upon the scene at the very last minute, having come from Oxford by a late train.

Mildred had taken care that neither Lord Wensleydown or Hector should be anywhere near Theodora. She had secured Lord Bracondale for herself, and did her best all through the repast to fascinate him.

And while he answered gallantly and paid her the grossest compliments, she knew he was laughing in his sleeve all the time, and it made her venom rise higher and higher.

Patrick Fitzgerald, the younger, was a dissipated, vicious youth, with his mother's faded coloring and none of the Fitzgerald charm. How infinitely her father surpassed any of the family she had seen yet, Theodora thought.

She did not enjoy her dinner. The youth's conversation was not interesting. But it was not until the ladies left the dining-room that her real penance began.

It seemed as if all the women crowded to one end of the drawing-room round Lady Harrowfield, and talked and whispered to one another, not one making way for Theodora or showing any knowledge of her presence. Barbara had gone off up to her room. She was too frightened of Mildred to disobey her, and she felt she would rather not be there to see their hateful ways to the dear, little, gentle cousin whom she thought she could love so much.

Theodora subsided on a sofa, wondering to herself if these were the manners of the great world in general. She hoped not; but although no human creature could be quite happy under the circumstances, she was not greatly distressed until she distinctly caught the name of "Mr. Brown" from the woman Josiah had taken in amid a burst of laughter, and saw Mildred, with a glance at her, ostentatiously suppress the speaker, who then continued her narration in almost a whisper, amid mocking titters of mirth.

Then anger burned in Theodora's gentle soul. They were talking about Josiah, of course, and turning him into ridicule.

She wondered, what would be the best to do. She was too far away to attempt to join in the conversation, or to be even able to swear she had heard aright, although there was no doubt in her own mind about it.

So she sat perfectly still on her great sofa, her hands folded in her lap, while two bright spots of wild rose flushed her cheeks.

She did not even pick up a book. There she sat like an alabaster statue, and most of the women were conscious of the exquisitely beautiful picture she made.

They could not stand in this packed group all the time, the whole dozen or more of them, and they gradually broke up into twos and threes about the large room.

They were delightfully friendly with one another, and all seemed in the best of spirits and tempers.

Most of them had no ulterior motive in their behavior to Theodora; it was merely the feeling that they were not the hostess and responsible. It was none of their business if Ada neglected her guests, and they all knew plenty of people and did not care to enlarge their acquaintance gratuitously.

So when they came in from the dining-room more than one of the men understood the picture they saw, of the beautiful, little, strange lady seated alone, while the other women chatted together in groups.

Hector was feeling irritated and excited, and longing to get near Theodora. He guessed Lord Wensleydown would have the same desire, and had no intention of being interfered with. He felt he could not bear to spend an evening watching the little brute daring to lean over her. He should kill him, or commit some violence, he knew.

Thus prudence, which at another time would have held him—would have made him remember what was best for her among this crowd of hostile women—flew to the winds. He must go to her—must show her he loved and would protect her, and, above all, that he would permit no other man to usurp his place.

And Theodora, who had been suffering silently a miserable feeling of loneliness and neglect, felt her heart bound with joy at the sight of his loved, familiar face, and she welcomed him more warmly than she had ever done before.

"Have these demons of women been odious to you, darling?" he whispered, hardly conscious of the term of endearment he had used. "Do not mind them; it is only jealousy because you are so beautiful and young."

"They have not been anything at all," she said, softly; "they have just left me alone and kept to themselves, and—and laughed at Josiah, and that has made me very angry, because—what has he done to them?"

"I loathe them all!" said Hector. "They are hardly fit to be in the same room with you, dear queen—and if you really belonged to me I would take you away from them now—to-night."

His voice was a caress, and that sentence, "belonged to me," always made her heart beat with its pictured possibilities. Oh, how she loved him! Could anything else in the world really matter while he could sit there and she could feel his presence and hear his tender words?

And so they talked awhile, and then they looked up and surveyed the scene. Josiah had been joined by Sir Patrick, and they were earnestly conversing by the fireplace. One or two pairs sat about on the sofas; but the general company showed signs of flocking off to the bridge-tables, which were laid out in another drawing-room beyond. And the couples joined them gradually, until only Lord Wensleydown and Morella Winmarleigh remained near and watched them with mocking eyes.

Hector had never before realized that Morella could have so much expression in her face.

How could he ever have thought under any conceivable circumstances, even at the end of his life, it would be possible to marry her! How thankful he felt he had never paid her any attention, or from his behavior given color to his mother's hopes.

He remembered a fairy story he had read in his youth, where a magic power was given to the hero of discovering what beast each human being was growing into by grasping their hands. And he wondered, if the gift had been his, what he should now find was the destiny of those two in front of him!

Wensleydown, no doubt, would be a great, sensual goat and Morella a vicious mule. And the idea made him laugh as he turned to Theodora again, to feast his eyes on her pure loveliness.

The Crow, who had arrived late and been among the last to enter the drawing-room before dinner, had not yet had an opportunity of speaking to Mrs. Brown, as he had been dragged off among the first of the bridge-players.

Presently Mildred looked through the door from the room beyond and called: "Freddy and Morella, come and play; we must have two more to make up the numbers. Uncle Patrick will bring Lord Bracondale presently."

Josiah and Theodora did not count at all, it seemed!

"What intolerable insolence!" said Hector, through his teeth. "I shall not play bridge or stir from here."

And Lord Wensleydown called back: "Do give one a moment to digest one's dinner, dear Lady Mildred. Miss Winmarleigh does not want to come yet, either. We are very—interested—and happy here."

Morella tittered and played with her fan. The dull, slow rage was simmering within her. Even her vanity could not misinterpret the meaning of Hector's devotion to Mrs. Brown. He was deeply in love, of course, and she, Morella, was robbed of her hopes of being Lady Bracondale. Her usually phlegmatic nature was roused in all its narrow strength. She was like some silent, vengeful beast waiting a chance to spring.

And so the evening wore away. Sir Patrick drew Josiah into the bridge-room, and made him join one of the tables where they were waiting for a fourth—Josiah, who was a very bad player, and did not really care for cards! But luck favored him, and the woman opposite restrained the irritable things she had ready to say to him when she first perceived how he played his hand.

And all the while Hector sat by Theodora, and learned more and more of her fair, clear mind. All the thoughts she had upon every subject he found were just and quaint and in some way illuminating. It was her natural sweetness of nature which made the great charm—that quality which Mrs. McBride had remarked upon, and which every one felt sooner or later.

Nothing of the ascetic saint or goody *poseuse*. She did not walk about with a book of poems under her arm, and wear floppy clothes and talk about her own and other people's souls. She was just human and true and attractive.

Theodora had perhaps no religion at all from the orthodox point of view; but had she been a Mohommedan or a Confucian or a Buddhist, she would still have been Theodora, full of gentleness and goodness and grace.

The entire absence of vanity and self-consciousness in her prevented her from feeling hurt or ruffled even with these ill-mannered women. She thought them rude and unpleasant, but they could not really hurt her except by humiliating Josiah. Her generosity instantly fired at that.

Both she and Hector perceived that Morella and Lord Wensleydown sat there watching them for no other reason but to disconcert and tease them, and it roused a spirit of resistance in both. While this was going on they would not move.

And Hector employed the whole of his self-control to keep himself from making actual love to her, and they talked of many things, and she understood and was grateful.

Presently, apparently, Morella could stand it no longer, for she rose rather abruptly and said to Lord Wensleydown:

"Come, let us play bridge."

They went on into the other room, and Theodora and Lord Bracondale were left quite alone.

"I should like to find Josiah," said Theodora. "Shall we not go, too?"

And they also followed upon the others' heels. Lady Ada happened to be out at her table, and some tardy sense of her duties as a hostess came to her, for she crossed over to where Theodora stood by the door and made some ordinary remark about hoping it would be fine on the morrow so they could enjoy the gardens.

And while she talked and looked into the blue eyes something attracted and softened her. She was very gentle and pretty, after all, the new niece, she decided, and Mildred had been quite wrong in saying she was an upstart and must be snubbed.

Lady Ada had a nervous way of blinking her light lashes in a fashion which suggested she might suffer from headache.

To Theodora she seemed a sad woman, full of cares, and she felt a kindly pity for her and no resentment for her rudeness.

Mildred looked up, and a frown of annoyance darkened her face.

The "creature" should certainly not make a conquest of her hostess if she could help it!

It was the first time Theodora had ever been into a company of people like this, and her eyes wandered over the scene when Lady Ada had to go back to her place.

"Tell me what you are thinking of?" said Hector, in her ear.

"I was thinking," she answered, "it is so interesting to watch people's faces. It seems to me so queer a way to spend one's time, the whole of one's intelligence set upon a game of cards and a few pieces of money for hours and hours together."

"They don't look attractive, do they?" he laughed.

"No, they look haggard, and worried, and old," she said. "Even the young ones look old and watchful, and so intent and solemn."

Lady Harrowfield had been losing heavily, and a deep mauve shade glowed through all her paint. She was a bad loser, and made all at her table feel some of her chagrin and wrath. In fact, candidates for the light of her smile found it advisable to let her win when things became too unpleasant.

There was a dreary silence over the room, broken by the scoring and remarks upon the games, and those who were out wandered into the saloon beyond, where iced drinks of all sorts were awaiting the weary.

"Every one must enjoy themselves how they can, of course," said Theodora. "It is absurd to try and make any one else happy in one's own way, but oh, I hope I shall not have to pass the time like that, ever! I don't think I could bear it."

The voices became raised at the table where Josiah sat. He had made some gross mistake in the game and his partner was being fretful over it. Her complaints amounted to real rudeness when the counting began. She had lost twenty pounds on this rubber, all through his last foolish play, she let it be known.

Josiah was angry with himself and deeply humiliated. He apologized as well as he could, but to no purpose with the wrathful dame.

And Theodora slipped behind his chair, and laid her hand upon his shoulder in what was almost a caress, and said, in a sweet and playful voice:

"You are a naughty, stupid fellow, Josiah, and of course you must pay the losses of both sides to make up for being such a wicked thing," and she patted his shoulders and smiled her gentle smile at the angry lady, as though they were children playing for counters or sweets, and the twenty pounds was a nothing to her husband, as indeed it was not. Josiah would cheerfully have paid a hundred to finish the unpleasant scene.

He was intensely grateful to her—grateful for her thought for him and for her public caress.

And the lady was so surprised at the turn affairs had taken that she said no more, and, allowing him to pay without too great protest, meekly suggested another rubber. But Josiah was not to be caught again. He rose, and, saying good-night, followed his wife and Lord Bracondale into the saloon.

XXV

After the rain and gloom of the week, Sunday dawned gloriously fine. There was to be a polo match on Monday in the park, which contained an excellent ground—Patrick and his Oxford friends against a scratch team. The neighborhood would watch them with interest. But the Sunday was for rest and peace, so all the morning the company played croquet, or lay about in hammocks, and more than half of them again began bridge in the great Egyptian tent which served as an out-door lounge on the lawn. It was reached from the western side down wide steps from the terrace, and beautiful rose gardens stretched away beyond.

Theodora had spent a sleepless night. There was no more illusion left to her on the subject of her feelings. She knew that each day, each hour, she was growing more deeply to love Hector Bracondale. He absorbed her thoughts, he dominated her imagination. He seemed to mean the only thing in life. The situation was impossible, and must end in some way. How could she face the long months with Josiah down at their new home, with the feverish hopes and fears of meetings! It was too cruel, too terrible; and she could not lead such a life. She had thought in Paris it would be possible, and even afford a certain amount of quiet happiness, if they could be strong enough to remain just friends. But now she knew this was not in human nature. Sooner or later fate would land them in some situation of temptation too strong for either to resist—and then—and then—She refused to face that picture. Only she writhed as she lay there and buried her face in the fine pillows. She did not permit herself any day-dreams of what might have been. Romauld himself, as he took his vows, never fought harder to regain his soul from the keeping of Claremonde than did Theodora to suppress her love for Hector Bracondale. Towards morning, worn out with fatigue, she fell asleep, and in her dreams, released from the control of her will, she spent moments of passionate bliss in his arms, only to wake and find she must face again the terrible reality. And cruellest thought of all was the thought of Josiah.

She had so much common-sense she realized the position exactly about him. She had not married him under any false impression. There had been no question of love—she had frankly been bought, and had as frankly detested him. But his illness and suffering had appealed to her tender heart—and afterwards his generosity. He was not unselfish, but, according to his lights, he heaped her with kindness. He could not help being common and ridiculous. And he had paid with solid gold for her, gold to make papa comfortable and happy, and she must fulfil her part of the bargain and remain a faithful wife at all costs.

This visit must be the last time she should meet her love. She must tell him, implore him—he who was free and master of his life; he must go away, must promise not to follow her, must help her to do what was right and just. She had no sentimental feeling of personal wickedness now. How could it be wicked to love—to love truly and tenderly? She had not sought love; he had come upon her. It would be wicked to give way to her feelings, to take Hector for a lover; but she had no sense of being a wicked woman as things were, any more than if she had badly burned her hand and was suffering deeply from the wound; she would have considered herself wicked for having had the mischance thus to injure herself. She was intensely unhappy, and she was going to try and do what was right. That was all. And God and those kind angels who steered the barks beyond the rocks would perhaps help her.

Hector for his part, had retired to rest boiling with passion and rage, the subtle, odious insinuations of Mildred ringing in his ears. The remembrance of the menace on Morella's dull face as she had watched Theodora depart, and, above all, Wensleydown's behavior as they all said good-night: nothing for him actually to take hold of, and yet enough to convulse him with jealous fury.

Oh, if she were only his own! No man should dare to look at her like that. But Josiah had stood by and not even noticed it.

Passionate jealousy is not a good foster-parent for prudence.

The Sunday came, and with it a wild, mad longing to be near her again—never to leave her, to prevent any one else from so much as saying a word. Others besides Wensleydown had begun to experience the attraction of her beauty and charm. If considerations of wisdom should keep him from her side, he would have the anguish of seeing these others take his place, and that he could not suffer.

And as passion in a man rages higher than in the average woman, especially passion when accelerated by the knowledge of another's desire to rob it of its own, so Hector's conclusions were not so clear as Theodora's.

He dared not look ahead. All he was conscious of was the absolute determination to protect her from Wensleydown—to keep her for himself.

And fate was gathering all the threads together for an inevitable catastrophe, or so it seemed to the Crow when the long, exquisite June Sunday evening was drawing to a close and he looked back on the day.

He would have to report to Anne that the two had spent it practically together; that Morella had a sullen red look on her face which boded ill for the part she would play, when she should be asked to play some part; that Mildred had done her best to render Theodora uncomfortable and unhappy, and thus had thrown her more into Hector's protection. The other women had been indifferent or mocking or amused, and Lady Harrowfield had let it be seen she would have no mercy. Her comments had been vitriolic.

Hector and Theodora had not gone out of sight, or been any different to the others; only he had never left her, and there could be no mistaking the devotion in his face.

For the whole day Sir Patrick had more or less taken charge of Josiah. He was finding him more difficult to manipulate over money matters than he had anticipated. Josiah's vulgar, round face and snub nose gave no index to his shrewdness; with his mutton-chop whiskers and bald head, Josiah was the personification of the smug grocer.

As she went to dress for dinner it seemed to Theodora that her heart was breaking. She was only flesh and blood after all, and she, too, had felt her pulses throbbing wildly as they had walked along by the lake, when all the color and lights of the evening helped to excite her imagination and exalt her spirit. They had been almost alone, for the other pair who composed the *partie carrée* of this walk were several yards ahead of them.

Each minute she had been on the verge of imploring him to say good-bye—to leave her—to let their lives part, to try to forget, and the words froze on her lips in the passionate, unspoken cry which seemed to rise from her heart that she loved him. Oh, she loved him! And so she had not spoken.

There had been long silences, and each was growing almost to know the other's thoughts—so near had they become in spirit.

When she got to her room her knees were trembling. She fell into a chair and buried her face in her hands. She shivered as if from cold.

Josiah was almost angry with her for being so late for dinner. Theodora hardly realized with whom she went in; she was dazed and numb. She got through it somehow, and this night determined to go straight to her room rather than be treated as she had been the night before. But one of the women whom the intercourse of the day had drawn into conversation with her showed signs of friendliness as they went through the anteroom, and drew her towards a sofa to talk. She was fascinated by Theodora's beauty and grace, and wanted to know, too, just where her clothes came from, as she did not recognize absolutely the models of any of the well-known *couturières*, and they were certainly the loveliest garments worn by any one in the party.

One person draws another, and soon Theodora had three or four around her—all purring and talking frocks. And as she answered their questions with gentle frankness, she wondered what everything meant. Did any of them feel—did any of them love passionately as she did?—or were they all dolls more or less bored and getting through life? And would she, too, grow like them in time, and be able to play bridge with interest until the small hours?

Later some of the party danced in the ballroom, which was beyond the saloon the other way, and now a definite idea came to Hector as he held Theodora in his arms in the waltz. They could not possibly bear this life. Why should he not take her away—away from the smug grocer, and then they could live their life in a dream of bliss in Italy, perhaps, and later at Bracondale. He had a great position, and people soon forget nowadays.

His pulses were bounding with these wild thoughts, born of their nearness and the long hours of strain. To-morrow he would tell her of them, but to-night—they would dance.

And Theodora felt her very soul melt within her. She was worn out with conflicting emotions. She could not fight with inclination any longer. Whatever he should say she would have to listen to—and agree with. She felt almost faint. And so at the end of the first dance she managed to whisper:

"Hector, I am tired. I shall go to bed." And in truth when he looked at her she was deadly white.

She stopped by her husband.

"Josiah," she said, "will you make my excuses to Lady Ada and Uncle Patrick? I do not feel well; I am going to my room."

Hector's distress was intense. He could not carry her up in his arms as he would have wished, he could not soothe and pet and caress her, or do anything in the world but stand by and see Josiah fussing and accompanying her to the stairs and on to her room. She hardly said the word good-night to him, and her very lips were white. Wensleydown's face, as he stood with Mildred, drove him mad with its mocking leer, and if he had heard their conversation there might have been bloodshed.

Josiah returned to the saloon, and made his way to the bridge-room to Sir Patrick and his hostess; but Hector still leaned against the door.

"He'll probably go out on the terrace and walk in the night by himself," thought the Crow, who had watched the scene, "and these dear people will say he has gone to meet her, and it is a ruse her being ill. They could not let such a chance slip, if they are both absent together."

So he walked over to Hector and engaged him in conversation.

Hector would have thought of this aspect himself at another time, but to-night he was dazed with passion and pain.

"Come and smoke a cigar on the terrace, Crow," he said. "One wants a little quiet and peace sometimes."

And then the Crow looked at him with his head on one side in that wise way which had earned for him his sobriquet.

"Hector, old boy, you know these damned people here and their ways. Just keep yourself in evidence, my son," he said, as he walked away.

And Hector thanked him in his heart, and went across and asked Morella to dance.

Up in her room Theodora lay prostrate. She could reason no more—she could only sob in the dark.

Next day she did not appear until luncheon-time. But the guests at Beechleigh always rose when they pleased, and no one remarked her absence even, each pair busy with their own affairs. Only Barbara crept up to her room to see how she was, and if she wanted anything. Theodora wondered why her cousin should have been so changed from the afternoon of their arrival. And Barbara longed to tell her. She moved about, and looked out of the window, and admired Theodora's beautiful hair spread over the pillows. Then she said:

"Oh, I wish you came here often and Mildred didn't. She is a brute, and she hates you for being so beautiful. She made me keep away, you know. Do you think me a mean coward?" Her poor, plain, timid face was pitiful as she looked at Theodora, and to her came the thought of what Barbara's life was probably among them all, and she said, gently:

"No, indeed, I don't. It was much better for you not to annoy her further; she might have been nastier to me than even she has been. But why don't you stand up for yourself generally? After all, you are Uncle Patrick's daughter, and she is only your mother's niece."

"They both love her far more than they do me," said Barbara, with hanging head.

And then they talked of other things. Barbara adored her home, but her family had no sentiment for it, she told Theodora; and Pat, she believed, would like to sell the whole thing and gamble away the money.

Just before luncheon-time, when Theodora was dressed and going down, Josiah came up again to see her. He had fussed in once or twice before during the morning. This time it was to tell her a special messenger had come from his agent in London to inform him his presence was absolutely necessary there the first thing on Tuesday morning. Some turn of deep importance to his affairs had transpired during the holiday. So he would go up by an early train. He had settled it all with Sir Patrick, who, however, would not hear of Theodora's leaving.

"The party does not break up until Wednesday or Thursday, and we cannot lose our greatest ornament," he had said.

"I do not wish to stay alone," Theodora pleaded. "I will come with you, Josiah."

But Josiah was quite cross with her.

"Nothing of the kind," he said. These people were her own relations, and if he could not leave her with them it was a strange thing! He did not want her in London, and she could join him again at Claridge's on Thursday. It would give him time to run down to Bessington to see that all was ready for her reception. He was so well now he looked forward to a summer of pleasure and peace.

"A second honeymoon, my love!" he chuckled, as he kissed her, and would hear no more.

And having planted this comforting thought for her consolation he had quitted the room.

Left alone Theodora sank down on the sofa. Her trembling limbs refused to support her; she felt cold and sick and faint.

A second honeymoon. Oh, God!

XXVI

At luncheon, when Theodora descended from her room, the whole party were assembled and already seated at the several little tables. The only vacant place left was just opposite Hector.

And there they faced each other during the meal, and all the time her eyes reminded him of the wounded fawn again, only they were sadder, if possible, and her face was pinched and pale, not the exquisite natural white of its usual fresh, soft velvet.

Something clutched at his heart-strings. What extra sorrow had happened to her since last night? What could he do to comfort and protect her? There was only one way—to take her with him out of it all.

After the first nine days' wonder, people would forget. It would be an undefended suit when Josiah should divorce her, and then he would marry her and have her for his very own. And what would they care for the world's sneers?

His whole being was thrilled and exalted with these thoughts; his brain was excited as with strong wine.

To have her for his own!

Even the memory of his mother only caused him a momentary pang. No one could help loving Theodora, and she—his mother—would get over it, too, and learn her sweetness and worth.

He was wildly happy now that he had made up his mind—so surely can passionate desire block out every other feeling.

The guests at their table were all more or less civil. Theodora's unassuming manner had disarmed them, and as savage beasts had been charmed of old by Orpheus and his lute, so perhaps her gentle voice had soothed this company—the women, of course; there had been no question of the men from the beginning.

Mildred's programme to make Mrs. Brown suffer was not having the success her zeal in promoting it deserved.

The weather was still glorious, and after lunch the whole party flocked out on the terrace.

A terrible nervous fear was dominating Theodora. She could not be alone with Hector, she did not dare to trust herself. And there would be the tomorrow and the Wednesday—without Josiah—and the soft warmth of the evenings and the glamour of the nights.

Oh, everything was too cruel and impossible! And wherever she turned she seemed to see in blazing letters, "A second honeymoon!"

The first was a horrible, fearsome memory which was over long ago, but the thought of a second—now that she knew what love meant, and what life with the loved one might mean—Oh, it was unbearable—terrible—impossible! better, much better, to die and have done with it all.

She kept close to Barbara, and when Barbara moved she feverishly engaged the Crow in conversation—any one—something to save her from any chance of listening to Hector's persuasive words. And the Crow's kind heart was pained by the hunted expression in her eyes. They seemed to ask for help and sanctuary.

"Shall we walk down to the polo-field, Mrs. Brown?" he said, and she gladly acquiesced and started with him.

If she had been a practised coquette she could not have done anything more to fan the flame of Hector's passion.

Lady Harrowfield had detained him on the top of the steps, and he saw her go off with the Crow and was unable to rush after them.

And when at last he was free he felt almost drunk with passion.

He had learned of Josiah's intended departure on the morrow, and that Theodora would join him again on the Thursday, and his mind was made up. On Wednesday night he would take her away with him to Italy. She should never belong to Josiah any more. She was his in soul and mind already, he knew, and she should be his in body, too, and he would cherish and love and protect her to the end of his life.

Every detail of his plan matured itself in his brain. It only wanted her consent, and that, when opportunity should be given him to plead his cause, he did not greatly fear would be refused.

Hitherto he had ever restrained himself when alone with her, had dominated his desire to make love to her; had never once, since Paris, given way to passion or tender words during their moments together.

But he remembered that hour of bliss on the way from Versailles; he remembered how she had thrilled, too, how he had made her feel and respond to his every caress.

Yes—she was not cold, his white angel!

He was playing in the scratch team of the polo match, and the wild excitement of his thoughts, coursing through his blood, caused him to ride like a mad thing.

Never had he done so brilliantly.

And Theodora, while she was every now and then convulsed with fear for him, had moments of passionate admiration.

The Crow remained at her side in the tent. He knew Hector would not be jealous of him, and the instinct of the brink of calamity was strong upon him, from the look in Theodora's eyes.

He used great tact—he turned the conversation to Anne and the children, and then to Lady Bracondale and Hector's home, all in a casual, abstract way, and he told her of Lady Bracondale's great love for her son, and of her hopes that he would marry soon, and how that Hector would be the last of his race—for Evermond Le Mesurier did not count—and many little tales about Bracondale and its people.

It was all done so wisely and well; not in the least as a note of warning. And all he said sank deep into Theodora's heart. She had never even dreamed of the plan which was now matured in Hector's brain—of going away with him. He, as really a lover, was not for her, that was a foregone conclusion. It was the fear of she knew not what which troubled her. She was too unsophisticated and innocent to really know—only that to be with him now was a continual danger; soon she knew she would not be able to control herself, she must be clasped in his arms.

And then—and then—there was the picture in front of her of Josiah and the "second honeymoon."

Thus while she sat there gazing at the man she passionately loved playing polo, she was silently suffering all the anguish of which a woman's heart is capable.

The only possible way was to part from Hector forever—to say the last good-bye before she should go, like a sheep, to the slaughter.

When she was once more the wife of Josiah she could never look upon his face again.

And if Hector had known the prospect that awaited her at Bessington Hall, it would have driven him—already mad—to frenzy.

The day wore on, and still Theodora's fears kept her from allowing a tête-à-tête when he dismounted and joined them for tea.

But fate had determined otherwise. And as the soft evening came several of the party walked down by the river—which ran on the western side below the rose-gardens and the wood of firs—to see Barbara's many breeds of ducks and water-fowl.

Then Hector's determination to be alone with her conquered for the time. Theodora found herself strolling with him in a path of meeting willows, with a summer-house at the end, by the water's bank.

They were quite separated from the others by now. They, with affairs of their own to pursue, had spread in different directions.

And it was evening, and warm, and June.

There was a strange, weird silence between them, and both their hearts were beating to suffocation—hers with the thought of the anguish of parting forever, his with the exaltation of the picture of parting no more.

They came to the little summer-house, and there they sat down and surveyed the scene. The evening lights were all opalescent on the water, there was peace in the air and brilliant fresh green on the trees, and soft and liquid rose the nightingale's note. So at last Hector broke the silence.

"Darling," he said, "I love you—I love you so utterly this cannot go on. I must have you for my own—" and then, as she gasped, he continued in a torrent of passionate words.

He told her of his infinite love for her; of the happiness he would fill her life with; of his plan that they should go away together when she should leave Beechleigh; of the joy of their days; of the tender care he would take of her; and every and each sentence ended with a passionate avowal of his love and devotion.

Then a terrible temptation seized Theodora. She had never even dreamed of this ending to the situation; and it would mean no second honeymoon of loathsome hours, but a glorious fulfilment of all possible joy.

For one moment the whole world seemed golden with happiness; but it was only of short duration. The next instant she remembered Josiah and her given word.

No, happiness was not for her. Death and sleep were all she could hope for; but she must not even hope for them. She must do what was right, and be true to herself, *advienne que pourra*. And perhaps some angel would give her oblivion or let her drink of Lethe, though she should never reach those waters beyond the rocks.

He saw the exaltation in her beautiful face as he spoke, and wild joy seized him. Then he saw the sudden droop of her whole body and the light die out of her eyes, and in a voice of anguish he implored her:

"Darling, darling! Won't you listen to what I say to you? Won't you answer me, and come with me?"

"No, Hector," she said, and her voice was so low he had to bend closer to hear.

He clasped her to his side, he covered her face with kisses, murmuring the tenderest love-words.

She did not resist him or seek to escape from his sheltering, strong arms. This was the end of her living life, why should she rob herself of a last joy?

She laid her head on his shoulder, and there she whispered in a voice he hardly recognized, so dominated it was by sorrow and pain: "It must be good-bye, beloved; we must not meet. Ah! never any more. I have been meaning to say this to you all the day. I cannot bear it either. Oh, we must part, and it must end; but oh, not—not in that way!"

He tried to persuade her, he pleaded with her, drew pictures of their happiness that surely would be, talked of Italy and eternal summer and exquisite pleasure and bliss.

And all the time he felt her quiver in his arms and respond to each thought, as her imagination took fire at the beautiful pictures of love and joy. But nothing shook her determination.

At last she said: "Dearest, if I were different perhaps, stronger and braver, I could go away and live with you like that, and keep it all a glorious thing; but I am not—only a weak creature, and the memory of my broken word, and Josiah's sorrow, and your mother's anguish, would kill all joy. We could have blissful moments of forgetfulness, but the great ghost of remorse would chase for me all happiness away. Dearest, I love you so; but oh, I could not live, haunted like that; I should just—die."

Then he knew all hope was over, and the mad passion went out of him, and his arms dropped to his sides as if half life had fled. She looked up in his face in fear at its ghastly whiteness.

And at this moment, through the parted willows, there appeared the sullen, mocking eyes of Morella Winmarleigh.

She pushed the bushes aside, and, followed by Lord Wensleydown, she came towards the summer-house.

Her slow senses had taken in the scene. Hector was evidently very unhappy, she thought, and that hateful woman had been teasing him, no doubt.

Thus her banal mind read the tragedy of these two human lives.

XXVII

Morella Winmarleigh had been taking an evening stroll with Lord Wensleydown. They had come upon the two in the summer-house quite by accident, but now they had caught them they would stick to them, and make their walk as tiresome as possible, they both decided to themselves.

After very great emotion such as Hector and Theodora had been experiencing, to have this uncongenial and hateful pair as companions was impossible to bear.

Neither Hector or Theodora stirred or made room for them on the seat.

"Isn't this a sweet place, Lord Wensleydown?" Miss Winmarleigh said. "Why have you never brought me here before? How did you find it, Hector?" turning to him in a determined fashion. "You will have to show us the way back, as we are quite lost!" and she giggled irritatingly.

"The first turn to the right at the end of the willows," said Hector, with what politeness he could summon up, "and I am sure you will be able to get to the house quite safely. As you are in such a hurry, don't let us keep you. Mrs. Brown and I are going the other way by the river, when we do start."

"Oh, we are not in a hurry at all," said Lord Wensleydown. "Do come with us, Mrs. Brown, we are feeling so lonely."

Theodora rose. She could bear no more of this.

"Let us go," she said to Hector, and they started, leading the way. And for a while they heard the others in mocking titters behind them, but presently, when near the house, they quickened their pace, and were again alone and free from their tormentors.

They had not spoken at all in this hateful walk, and now he turned to her.

"My darling," he said, "life seems over for me."

"And for me, too, Hector," she said. "And when we come to this dark piece of wood I want you to kiss me once more and say good-bye forever, and go out of my life." There was a passionate sob in her voice. "And oh! *Bien-aimé*, please promise me you will leave to-morrow. Do not make it more impossible to bear than it already is."

But he was silent with pain. A mad, reckless revolt at fate flooded all his being.

It was past eight o'clock now, and when they came to the soothing gloom of the dark firs he crushed her in his arms, and a great sob broke from him and rent her heart.

"My darling, my darling! Good-bye," he said, brokenly. "You have taught me all that life means; all that it can hold of pleasure and pain. Henceforth, it is the gray path of shadows; and oh, God take care of you and grant us some peace."

But she was sobbing on his breast and could not speak.

"And remember," he went on, "I shall never forget you or cease to worship and adore you. Always know you have only to send me a message, a word, and I will come to you and do what you ask, to my last drop of blood. I love you! Oh, God! I love you, and you were made for me, and we could have been happy together and glorified the world."

Then he folded her again in his arms and held her so close it seemed the breath must leave her body, and then they walked on silently, and silently entered the house by the western garden door.

The evening was a blank to Theodora. She dressed in her satins and laces, and let her maid fasten her wonderful emeralds on throat and breast and hair. She descended to the drawing-room and walked in to dinner with some strange man—all as one in a dream. She answered as an automaton, and the man thought how beautiful she was, and what a pity for so beautiful a woman to be so stupid and silent and dull.

"Almost wanting," was his last comment to himself as the ladies left the dining-room.

Then Theodora forced herself to speak—to chatter to a now complacent group of women who gathered round her. Those emeralds, and the way the diamonds were set round them, proved too strong an attraction for even Lady Harrowfield to keep far away.

She was going to have her rubies remounted, and this seemed just the pattern she would like.

So the time passed, and the men came into the room. But Hector was not with them. He had found a telegram, it transpired, which had been waiting for him on his return, and it would oblige him to go to Bracondale immediately, so he was motoring up to London that night. He had acted his part to the end, and no one guessed he was leaving the best of his life behind him. When Theodora realized he was gone she suddenly felt very faint; but she, too, was not of common clay, and breeding will tell in crises of this sort, so she sat up and talked gayly. The evening passed, and at last she was alone for the night.

There are moralists who will assure us the knowledge of having done right brings its own consolation. And in good books, about good women, the heroine experiences a sense of peace and satisfaction after having resigned the forbidden joy of her life. But Theodora was only a human being, so she spent the night in wild, passionate regret.

She had done right with no stern sense of the word "Right" written up in front of her, but because she was so true and so sweet that she must keep her word and not betray Josiah. She did not analyze anything. Life was over for her, whatever came now could only find her numb. By an early train Josiah left for London.

"Take care of yourself, my love," he had said, as he looked in at her door, "and write to me this afternoon as to what train you decide to leave by on Thursday."

She promised she would, and he departed, thoroughly satisfied with his visit among the great world.

The day was spent as the other days, and after lunch Theodora escaped to her room. She must write her letter to Josiah for the afternoon's post. She had discovered the train left at eleven o'clock. It did not take her long, this little note to her husband, and then she sat and stared into space for a while.

The terrible reaction had begun. There was no more excitement, only the flatness, the blank of the days to look forward to, and that unspeakable sense of loss and void. And oh, she had let Hector go without one word of her passionate love! She had been too unnerved to answer him when he had said his last good-bye to her in the wood.

She seized the pen again which had dropped from her hand. She would write to him. She would tell him her thoughts—in a final farewell. It might comfort him, and herself, too.

So she wrote and wrote on, straight out from her heart, then she found she had only just time to take the letters to the hall.

She closed Hector's with a sigh, and picking up Josiah's, already fastened, she ran with them quickly down the stairs.

There was an immense pile of correspondence—the accumulation of Whitsuntide.

The box that usually received it was quite full, and several letters lay about on the table.

She placed her two with the rest, and turned to leave the hall. She could not face all the company on the lawn just yet, and went back to her room, meeting Morella Winmarleigh bringing some of her own to be posted as she passed through the saloon.

When Miss Winmarleigh reached the table curiosity seized her. She guessed what had been Theodora's errand. She would like to see her writing and to whom the letters were addressed.

No one was about anywhere. All the correspondence was already there, as in five minutes or less the post would go.

She had no time to lose, so she picked up the last two envelopes which lay on the top of the pile and read the first:

To
Josiah Brown, Esq.,
Claridge's Hotel,
Brook Street,
London, W.

and the other:

The Lord Bracondale,
Bracondale Chase,
Bracondale.

"The husband and—the lover!" she said to herself. And a sudden temptation came over her, swift and strong and not to be resisted.

Here would be revenge—revenge she had always longed for! while her sullen rage had been gathering all these last days. She heard the groom of the chambers approaching to collect the letters; she must decide at once. So she slipped Theodora's two missives into her blouse and walked towards the door.

"There is another post which goes at seven, isn't there, Edgarson?" she asked, "and the letters are delivered in London to-morrow morning just the same?"

"Yes, ma'am, they arrive by the second post in London," said the man, politely, and she passed on to her room.

Arrived there, excitement and triumph burned all over her. Here, without a chance of detection, she could crush her rival and see her thoroughly punished, and—who knows?—Hector might yet be caught in the rebound.

She would not hesitate a second. She rang for her maid.

"Bring me my little kettle and the spirit-lamp. I want to sip some boiling water," she said. "I have indigestion. And then you need not wait—I shall read until tea."

She was innocently settled on her sofa with a book when the maid returned. She was a well-bred servant, and silently placed the kettle and glass and left the room noiselessly. Morella sprang to her feet with unusual agility. Her heavy form was slow of movement as a rule.

The door once locked, she returned to the sofa and began operations.

The kettle soon boiled, and the steam puffed out and achieved its purpose.

The thin, hand-made paper of the envelope curled up, and with no difficulty she opened the flap.

Hector's letter first and then Josiah's. All her pent-up, concentrated rage was having its outlet, and almost joy was animating her being.

Hector's was a long letter; probably very loving, but that did not concern her.

It would be most unladylike to read it, she decided—a sort of thing only the housemaids would do. What she intended was to place them in the wrong envelopes—Hector's to Josiah, and Josiah's to Hector. It was a mistake any one might make themselves when they were writing, and Theodora, when it should be discovered, could only blame her own supposed carelessness. Even if the letter was an innocent one, which was not at all likely. Oh, dear, no! She knew the world, however little girls were supposed to understand. She had kept her eyes open, thank goodness; and it would certainly not be an epistle a husband would care to read—a great thing of pages and pages like that. But even if it were innocent, it was bound to cause some trouble and annoyance; and the thought of that was honey and balm to her.

She slipped them into the covers she had destined for them and pressed down the damp gum. So all was as it had been to outward appearance, and she felt perfectly happy. Then when she descended to tea she placed them securely in the box under some more of her own for the seven-o'clock post, and went her way rejoicing.

XXVIII

Next morning, over a rather late breakfast in his sitting-room at Claridge's, Josiah's second post came in.

All had gone well with his business in the City the day before, and in the afternoon he had run down to Bessington Hall, returning late at night.

He was feeling unusually well and self-important, and his thoughts turned to pleasant things: To the delight of having Theodora once more as a wife; of his hope of founding a family—the Browns of Bessington—why not? Had not a boy at the gate called him squire?

"Good-day to 'e, squire," he had said, and that was pleasant to hear.

If only his tiresome cough would keep off in the autumn, he might himself shoot the extensive coverts he had ordered to be stocked on the estate. He had heard there were schools for would-be sportsmen to learn the art of handling a gun, and he would make inquiries.

All the prospect was fair.

He picked up his letters and turned them over. Nothing of importance. Ah, yes! there was Theodora's. The first letter she had ever written him, and such a long one! What could the girl have to say? Surely not all that about trains! He opened the envelope with a knife which lay by his plate, and this is what he read—read with whitening face and sinking heart:

"BEECHLEIGH, *June 5th*.

"HECTOR, MY BELOVED!—Oh, for this last time I must think of you as that! Dearest, we are parted now and may never meet again, and the pain of it all kept me silent yesterday, when my heart was breaking with the anguish and longing to tell you how I loved you, how you were not going away suffering alone. Oh, it has all crept upon us, this great, great love! It was fate, and it was useless to struggle against it. Only we must not let it be the reason of our doing wrong—that would be to degrade it, and love should not live in an atmosphere of degradation. I could not go away with you, could not have you for my lover without breaking a bargain—a bargain over which I have given my word. Of course I did not know what love meant when I was married. In France one does not think of that as connected with a husband. It was just a duty to be got through to help papa and my sisters. But my part of the bargain was myself, and in return for giving that I have money and a home, and papa and Sarah and Clementine are comfortable and happy. And as Josiah has kept his side of it, so I must keep mine, and be faithful to him always in word and deed. Dearest, it is too terrible to think of this material aspect to a bond which now I know should only be one of love and faith and tenderness. But it *is* a bond, and I have given my word, and no happiness could come to us if I should break it, *as Josiah has not broken his*. And oh, Hector, you do not know how good he has always been to me, and generous and indulgent! It is not his fault that he is not of our class, and I must do my utmost to make him happy, and atone for this wound which I have unwittingly given him, and which he is, and must always remain, unconscious of. Oh, if something could have warned me, after that first time we met, that I would love you—had begun to love you—even then there would have been time to draw back, to save us both, perhaps, from suffering. And yet, and yet, I do not know, we might have missed the greatest and noblest good of all our lives. Dearest, I want you to keep the memory of me as something happy. Each year, when the spring-time comes and the young fresh green, I want you to look back on our day at Versailles, and to say to yourself, 'Life cannot be all sad, because nature gave the earth the returning spring.' And some> spring must come for us, too—if only in our hearts.

"And now, O my beloved, good-bye! I cannot even tell to you the anguish which is wringing my heart. It is all summed up in this. I love you! I love you! and we must say forever a farewell!

"THEODORA.

"P.S.—I am sending this to your home."

As he read the last words the paper slipped from Josiah's nerveless hands, and for many minutes he sat as one stricken blind and dumb. Then his poor, plebeian figure seemed to crumple up, and with an inarticulate cry of rage and despair he fell forward, with his head upon his out-stretched arms across the breakfast-table.

How long he remained there he never knew. It seemed a whole lifetime later when he began to realize things—to know where he was—to remember.

"Oh, God!" he said. "Oh, God!"

He picked up the letter and read it all over again, weighing every word.

Who was this thief who had stolen his wife? Hector? Hector? Yes, it was Lord Bracondale; he remembered now he had heard him called that at Beechleigh. He would like to kill him. But was he a thief, after all? or was not—he—Josiah the thief? To have stolen her happiness, and her life. Her young life that might have been so fair, though how did he know that at the time! He had never thought of such things. She was what he desired, and he had bought her with gold. No, he was not a thief, he had bought her with gold, and because of that she was going to keep to her bargain, and make him a true and faithful wife.

"Oh, God!" he said again. "Oh, God!"

Presently the business method of his life came back to him and helped him. He must think this matter over carefully and see if there was any way out. It all looked black enough—his future, that but an hour ago had seemed so full of promise. He rang for the waiter and gave orders to have the breakfast things taken away. That accomplished, he requested that he should not be disturbed upon any pretext whatsoever. And then, drawn up to his writing-table, he began deliberately to think.

Yes, from the beginning Theodora had been good and meek and docile. He remembered a thousand gentle, unselfish things she had done for him. Her patience, her kindness, her unfailing sympathy in all his ills, the consideration and respect with which she treated him. When—when could this thing have begun? In Paris? Only these short weeks ago—was love so sudden a passion as that? Then he turned to the letter again and once more read it through. Poor Theodora, poor little girl, he thought. His anger was gone now; nothing remained but an intolerable pain. And this lord—of her own class—her own class! How that thought hurt. What of him? He was handsome and young, and just the mate for Theodora. And she had said good-bye to him, and was going to do her best to make him—Josiah—happy. He gave a wild laugh. Oh, the mockery of it all, the mockery of it all! Well, if she could renounce happiness to keep her word, what could he do for her in return? She must never know of the mistake she had made in putting the letters into the wrong envelopes. That he could save her from. But the man? He would know—for he must have got the note intended for him—Josiah. What must be done about that? He thought and thought. And at last he drew a sheet of paper forward and wrote, in his neat, clerklike hand, just a few lines.

And these were they:

> "MY LORD,—You will have received, I presume, a communication addressed to you and intended for me. The enclosed speaks for itself. I send it to you because it is my duty to do so. If I were a young man, though I am not of your class, I would kill you. But I am growing old, and my day is over. All I ask of you is never, *under any circumstances*, to let my wife know of her mistake about the letters. I do not wish to grieve her, or cause her more suffering than you have already brought upon her.

"Believe me,
"Yours faithfully,
"JOSIAH BROWN."

Then he got down the *Peerage* and found the correct form of superscription he must place upon the envelope.

He folded the two letters, his own and Theodora's, and, slipping them in, sealed the packet with his great seal which was graven with a deep J.B. And lest he should change his mind, he rang the bell for the waiter, and had it despatched to the post at once—to be sent by express. If possible it must reach Lord Bracondale at the same time as the other letter—Theodora's letter to himself in the wrong envelope.

And then poor Josiah subsided into his chair again, and suffered and suffered. He was conscious of nothing else—just intense, overwhelming suffering.

When his secretary, from his office in the City, came in about luncheon-time to transact some important business, he was horrified and distressed to see the change in his patron; for Josiah looked crumpled and shrivelled and old.

"I caught a chill coming from Bessington last night," he explained, "and I will send for Toplington to give me a draught if you will kindly touch the bell."

Then he tried to concentrate his mind on his affairs and get through the day. But the gray look kept growing and growing, and the secretary decided towards evening to suggest sending for Theodora. Josiah, however, would not hear of this. He was not ill, he said, it was merely a chill; he would be quite restored by a night's rest, and Mrs. Brown would be with him, anyway, in the morning. Of what use to alarm her unnecessarily. But he had unfortunately mislaid her letter with the exact time of her train, so he had better telegraph to her before six o'clock to make sure. He wrote it out himself. Just:

"Stupidly mislaid your letter. What time did you say
for the carriage to meet your train? "JOSIAH."

And about eight o'clock her reply came, and then he went to bed, wondering if he had reached the summit of human suffering or if there would be more to come.

XXIX

Late that night, in the old panelled library at Bracondale, Hector walked up and down. He, too, was suffering, suffering intensely, his only grain of comfort being that he was alone. His mother was away in the north with Anne, and he had the place to himself. In his hand was Theodora's letter. As Josiah had calculated, knowing cross-country posts, both his and hers had arrived at the same time.

Hector paced and paced up and down, his thoughts maddening him.

And so three people were unhappy now—not he and his beloved one alone. This was the greater calamity.

But how he had misjudged Josiah! The common, impossible husband had behaved with a nobility, a justice, and forbearance which he knew his own passionate nature would not have been capable of. It had touched him to the core, and he had written at once in reply, enclosing Theodora's letter about the arrival of the train.

> "DEAR SIR,—I am overcome with your generosity and your justice. I thank you for your letter and for your magnanimity in forwarding the enclosure it contained. I understand and appreciate the sentiment you express when you say, had you been younger you would have killed me, and I on my side would have been happy to offer you any satisfaction you might have wished, and am ready to do so now if you desire it. At the same time, I would like you to know, in deed, I have never injured you. My deep and everlasting grief will be that I have brought pain and sorrow into the life of a lady who is very dear to us both. My own life is darkened forever as well, and I am going away out of England for a long time as soon as I can make my arrangements. I will respect your desire never to inform your wife of her mistake, and I will not trouble either of you again. Only, by a later post, I intend to answer her letter and say farewell.

"Believe me,
"Yours truly,
"BRACONDALE."

This he had despatched some hours ago, but his last good-bye to Theodora was not yet written. What could he say to her? How could he tell her of all the misery and anguish, all the pain which was racking his being; he, who knew life and most things it could hold, and so could judge of the fact that nothing, nothing, counted now but herself—and they should meet no more, and it was the end. A blank, absolute end to all joy. Nothing to exist upon but the remembrance of an hour or two's bliss and a few tender kisses.

And as Josiah had done, he could only say: "Oh, God! Oh, God!"

On top of his large escritoire there stood a minute and very perfect copy of the fragment of Psyche, which he had so intensely admired. He turned to it now as his only consolation; the likeness to Theodora was strong; the exact same form of face, and the way her hair grew; the pure line of the cheek, and the angle which the head was set on to the column of her throat—all might have been chiselled from her. How often had he seen her looking down like that. Perhaps the only difference at all was that Theodora's nose was fine, and not so heavy and Greek; otherwise he had her there in front of him—his Theodora, his gift of the gods, his Psyche, his soul. And wherever he should wander—if in wildest Africa or furthest India, in Alaska or Tibet—this little fragment of white marble should bear him company.

It calmed him to look at it—the beautiful Greek thing.

And he sat down and wrote to his loved one his good-bye.

What Could He Say to Her.

He told her of his sorrow and his love, and how he was going away from England, he did not yet know where, and should be absent many months, and how forever his thoughts from distant lands would bridge the space between them, and surround her with tenderness and worship.

And her letter, he said, should never leave him—her two letters; they should be dearer to him than his life. He prayed her to take care of herself, and if at any time she should want him to send for him from the ends of the earth. Bracondale would always find him, sooner or later, and he was hers to order as she willed.

And as he had ended his letter before, so he ended this one now:

"For ever and ever your devoted
"Lover."

After this he sat a long time and gazed out upon the night. It was very dark and cloudy, but in one space above his head two stars shone forth for a moment in a clear peep of sky, and they seemed to send him a message of hope. What hope? Was it, as she had said, the thought that there would be a returning spring—even for them?

XXX

And the summer wore away and the dripping autumn came, and with each week, each day almost, Josiah seemed to shrivel.

It was not very noticeable at first, after the ten days of sharp illness which had prostrated him when he received the fatal letter.

He appeared to recover almost from that, and they went down to Bessington Hall at the beginning of July. But there was no further talk of a second honeymoon.

Theodora's tenderness and devotion never flagged. If her heart was broken she could at least keep her word, and try to make her husband happy. And so each one acted a part, with much zeal for the other's welfare.

It was anguish to Josiah to see his wife's sweet face grow whiter and thinner; she was so invariably bright and cheerful with him, so considerate of his slightest wish.

His pride and affection for her had turned into a sort of adoration as the days wore on. He used to watch her silently from behind a paper, or when she thought he slept. Then the mask of smiles fell from her, and he saw the pathetic droop of her young, fair head and the mournful gloom that would creep into her great, blue eyes.

And he was the stumbling-block to her happiness. She had sent away the man she loved in order to stay and be true to him, to minister to his wants, and do her utmost to render him happy. Oh, what could he do for her in return? What possible thing?

He lavished gifts upon her; he lavished gifts upon her sisters, upon her father; their welfare, he remembered, was part of the bargain. At least she would know these—her dear ones—had gained by it, and, so far, her sacrifice had not been in vain.

This thought comforted him a little. But the constant gnawing ache at his heart, and the withdrawal of all object to live for, soon began to tell upon his always feeble constitution.

Of what use was anything at all? His house or his lands! His pride in his position—even his title of "squire," which he often heard now. All were dead-sea fruit, dust and ashes; there never would be any Browns of Bessington in the years to come. There never would be anything for him, never any more.

For a week in September Captain and Mrs. Dominic Fitzgerald had paid them a visit, and the brilliant bride had cheered them up for a little and seemed to bring new life with her. She expressed herself as completely satisfied with her purchase in the way of a husband; it was just as she had known, three was a lucky number for her, and Dominic was her soul's mate, and they were going to lead the life they both loved, of continual movement and change and gayety.

But the situation at Bessington distressed her.

"Why, my dear, they are just like a couple of sick paroquets," she said to her husband. "Mr. Brown don't look long for this world, and Theodora is a shadow! What in the Lord's name has been happening to them?"

But Dominic could not enlighten her. Before they left she determined to ascertain for herself.

The last evening she said to Theodora, who was bidding her good-night in her room:

"I had a letter from your friend Lord Bracondale last week, from Alaska. He asks for news of you. Did you see him after he came from Paris? He was only a short while in England, I understand."

"Yes, we saw him once or twice," said Theodora, "and we made the acquaintance of his sister."

"He always seemed to be very fond of her. Is she a nice sort of woman?"

"Very nice."

"I hear the mother is clean crazy with him for going off again and not marrying that heiress they are so set upon. But why should he? He don't want the money."

"No," said Theodora.

"Was he at Beechleigh when you were there?"

"Yes."

"And Miss Winmarleigh, too?"

"Yes, she was there."

"Oh!" said Mrs. Fitzgerald. "A great lump of a woman, isn't she?"

"She is rather large."

This was hopeless—a conversation of this sort—Jane Fitzgerald decided. It told her nothing.

Theodora's face had become so schooled it did not, even to her stepmother's sharp eyes, betray any emotion.

"I am glad if the folly is over," she thought to herself. "But I shouldn't wonder if it wasn't something to do with it still, after all. If it is not that, what can it be?" Then she said aloud: "He is going through America, and we shall meet him when we get back in November, most likely. I shall persuade him to come down to Florida with us, if I can. He seems to be aimlessly wandering round, I suppose, shooting things; but Florida is the loveliest place in the world, and I wish you and Josiah would come, too, my dear."

"That would be beautiful," said Theodora, "but Josiah is not fit for a long journey. We shall go to the Riviera, most probably, when the weather gets cold."

"Have you no message for him then, Theodora, when I see him?"

And now there was some sign. Theodora clasped her hands together, and she said in a constrained voice:

"Yes. Tell him I hope he is well—and I am well—just that," and she walked ever to the dressing-table and picked up a brush, and put it down again nervously.

"I shall tell him no such thing," said her step-mother, kindly, "because I don't believe it is true. You are not well, dear child, and I am worried about you."

But Theodora assured her that she was, and all was as it should be, and nothing further could be got out of her; so they kissed and wished each other good-night. And Jane Fitzgerald, left to herself, heaved a great sigh.

Next day, after this cheery pair had gone, things seemed to take a deeper gloom.

The mention of Hector's name and whereabouts had roused Theodora's dormant sorrows into activity again; and with all her will and determination to hide her anguish, Josiah could perceive an added note of pathos in her voice at times and less and less elasticity in her step.

Once he would have noticed none of these things, but now each shade of difference in her made its impression upon him.

And so the time wore on, their hearts full of an abiding grief.

When October set in Josiah caught a bad cold, which obliged him to keep to his bed for days and days. He did not seem very ill, and assured his wife he would be all right soon; but by November, Sir Baldwin Evans, who was sent for hurriedly from London, broke it gently to Theodora that her husband could not live through the winter. He might not even live for many days. Then she wept bitter tears. Had she been remiss in anything? What could she do for him? Oh, poor Josiah!

And Josiah knew that his day was done, as he lay there in his splendid, silk-curtained bed. But life had become of such small worth to him that he was almost glad.

"Now, soon she can be happy—my little girl," he said to himself, "with the one of her class. It does not do to mix them, and I was a fool to try. But her heart is too kind ever to quite forget poor old Josiah Brown."

And this thought comforted him. And that night he died.

Then Theodora wept her heart out as she kissed his cold, thin hand.

When they got the telegram in New York at Mrs. Fitzgerald's mansion, Hector was just leaving the house, and Captain Fitzgerald ran after him down the steps.

"My son-in-law, Josiah Brown, is dead," he said. "My wife thought you would be interested to hear. Poor fellow, he was not very old either—only fifty-two."

Hector almost staggered for a moment, and leaned against the gilded balustrade. Then he took off his hat reverently, while he said, in his deep, expressive voice:

"There lived no greater gentleman."

And Captain Fitzgerald wondered if he were mad or what he could mean, as he watched him stride away down the street.

But when he told his wife, she understood, for she had just learned from Hector the whole story.

And perhaps—who knows? Far away in Shadowland Josiah heard those words, "There lived no greater gentleman." And if he did—they fell like balm on his sad soul.

XXXI

It was eighteen months after this before they met again—Hector and Theodora; and now it was May, and the flowers bloomed and the birds sang, and all the world was young and fair—only Morella Winmarleigh was growing into a bitter old maid.

At twenty-eight people might have taken her for a matron of ten years older.

She had wondered for weeks what was the result of her action with the letters. She hoped daily to hear of some catastrophe and scandal falling upon the head of Theodora. But she heard nothing. It was only after Josiah's death that details were wafted to her through the Fitzgeralds.

How poor Mr. Brown had never really recovered from a slight stroke he had had on leaving Beechleigh, and of Theodora's goodness and devotion to him, and of his worship of her. And Morella had the maddening feeling that if she had left well alone this death might never have occurred, and her hated rival might not now be a free and beautiful widow, with no impediment between herself and Hector when they should choose to meet.

She had meant to be revenged and punish them, and it seemed she had only cleared their path to happiness. There was really no justice in this world!

Theodora had gone to meet her father and step-mother in Paris.

Her sisters were married and very happy, she hoped. Prosperity had wonderfully embellished their attractions, and even Sarah had found a mate.

And Lady Bracondale remained her placid, stately self. Her grief and disappointment over Hector's departure from England had passed away by now, as so had her treasured dream of receiving Morella Winmarleigh as a daughter. But Anne whispered to her that she need not worry forever, and some day soon her brother might choose a bride whom even she would love.

Hector had continued his wanderings over the world for many months after Josiah's death. He felt, should he return to England, nothing could keep him from Theodora.

And she, too, had travelled and explored fresh scenes, and was now a supremely beautiful and experienced woman—courted and flattered, and besieged by many adorers.

But she was still Theodora, with only one love in her heart and one dream in her soul—to meet Hector again and spend the rest of her life in the shelter of his arms.

She heard of him often through her step-mother; and sometimes she saw Anne—and both Hector and she understood, and knew the time would come when they could be happy.

Jane Anastasia Fitzgerald had romantic notions. This pretty pair, whom she looked upon as of her own producing, must meet again under her auspices in like circumstances as they had done on the happy and never-to-be-forgotten day when she herself had promised her heart and hand to Dominic Fitzgerald.

"There is something lucky about Versailles," she said, "and they shall experience it, too!"

So she planned a picnic, and arranged it with Hector before he reached Paris. He was not to show himself or communicate with Theodora; he was just to be there at the Réservoirs and wait for their arrival.

And the gods smiled—and the day was fine—and the trees were green—as had been another day, two years ago.

And oh, the wild, mad joy that surged up in their hearts when their eyes met once more!

They could not speak, it seemed, even the words of politeness; so they wandered away into the spring woods, silent and glad; and it was not until they reached the shrine of old Enceladus that Hector clasped Theodora again in his arms, and gave rein to all the passionate love and delirious happiness which was flooding his being.

There one can leave them—together—for always—looking out upon the realization of that fair dream of life.

Safe in each other's arms, in those smooth waters, beyond the rocks.

THE END

Milton Keynes UK
Ingram Content Group UK Ltd.
UKHW040040281223
435071UK00008B/707